SAM CRESCENT

EVERNIGHT PUBLISHING ®

www.evernightpublishing.com

Copyright© 2018

Sam Crescent

Editor: Karyn White

Cover Artist: Sour Cherry Designs

Jacket Design: Jay Aheer

ISBN: 978-1-77339-712-2

SAM CRESCENT

.

THE CLAIMING

The Pack Claims a Mate, 1

Sam Crescent

Copyright © 2013

Chapter One

Tom Snow glanced over at the bus stop. The scent coming off the voluptuous blonde woman was intoxicating. Licking his lips, he felt an answering pulse in his dick as he watched her flick hair off her shoulder. She was the one. The woman he'd been searching for, for over a decade. Feeling euphoric, he headed toward the mystery woman. She hadn't spotted him yet, which he was thankful for. Roy, Guy, Stuart, Mark, and Joey were all counting on him to find their one mate. Their time was running out, and he was feeling the desperate ache of the full moon. With each passing year and every full moon, Tom felt the calling of the wolf beast within him.

Her scent was everything he'd been hoping for. She was wild, unique, and utterly beautiful. His heart pounded as he approached. She hadn't seen him yet. The bus stop wasn't busy, but the woman in question was clicking away on her cell phone. She didn't look up even as he approached.

Standing beside her, Tom watched as she popped some gum as she continued to work on her phone. When he stood beside her, she finally looked up. She gave him a smile and went back to her phone.

"Is it me or are buses a pain in the ass?" she asked, giggling.

Fuck, his cock was going to tear through his jeans. Her voice was the thing of sweet, sex dreams.

Staring at her, he wondered how he could make her part of his pack. She glanced at him and frowned.

He checked around the street and saw it was practically deserted. Were the fates on his side? Taking a deep breath, he stepped closer to her.

"What are you doing?" she asked.

"How would you like to spend the night with me?" he asked.

She laughed. "You're not serious?"

"I'm more serious than you can believe." Stepping up close, he inhaled her scent. Fuck, she was the one! There was no way he could let her go. "You're the one," he said.

"Look, dude, I don't know what meds you're on, but you've got the wrong girl." She hitched her bag high on her shoulder and stepped away from him. The beast within him reacted. Before he could control what he was doing, Tom pulled her into the alley. He covered her mouth to stop her from screaming.

He expected her to be drowning in fear. What surprised him was the fact she wasn't terrified of him. Her scent was filled only with anger.

When he felt her stop fighting, Tom picked her up in his arms and carried her over to his truck. Fuck, he'd just kidnapped a human woman.

Slamming his fists against the steering wheel Tom tried to fight against his wolf. *Crap, fuck, shit, crap.* He couldn't believe he'd just kidnapped a woman. What the hell was he doing?

Not stopping the truck, he kept on driving until he was well on his way to his house in the middle of nowhere surrounded by layers of trees. The forests were deep and rich with deer and plenty of animals for them to hunt. They rarely entered the human world, but there were times it was necessary. Tom usually let Guy deal with everything in town, but for once he'd wanted to check everything out himself.

When he was on the path toward his home, Tom finally started to calm down. Humans never walked onto his land. They all kept their distance from him and his wolves. Guy and the twins were the only ones from his pack who tried to fit within the human world. He'd long ago stopped caring for easy sex and the connection with others. Tom had learned to accept he was a wolf, and with that came risks.

He saw his men stood outside the front door waiting for him.

Guy, Roy, and Stuart had their arms folded while Mark and Joey were fighting each other. They all stopped when he pulled the truck to a stop. Their bodies tensed as if they sensed he fucked up.

"What have you done?" Roy asked. Out of all of the wolves, Roy was the quietest and the most intelligent.

"I found her," Tom said, climbing down from the truck. He walked around to the other side, opened the truck and let her scent assail them.

Mark and Joey growled as their beasts took over. "She smells fucking beautiful."

"Why is she unconscious?" Roy asked, clearly ignoring her scent.

"I didn't know what else to do. She wouldn't have come." Tom lifted her into his arms and presented their mate to the rest of his pack. They were all his brothers with him being the eldest. Their parents died many years ago, leaving them alone to fend for themselves. Being the eldest had terrified Tom in the early days whereas now, he was well into his role as alpha. Roy was a couple years younger, with Guy, then Stuart coming next, and then the twins.

"You kidnapped a human woman?" Guy asked, catching onto Roy's questioning. They were running out of time. The beast within them was slowly taking hold until there would be nothing left. Their father had warned him about their curse. They were bound by the moon and would have until Tom reached thirty-five before the beast within them would become the dominant figure. If they didn't find the woman meant for them, on Tom's birthday they would all be bound to be wolves forever. Tom was thirty-five next year. With five brothers to be responsible for, Tom couldn't wait anymore. This woman was going to be theirs. She was their last option.

Their father didn't have any siblings and didn't have to worry about others turning into a beast once he was old enough. Tom wouldn't ruin his brothers' lives.

"We're running out of time," Tom said, gritting his teeth together to try to stop the fear coursing through his veins. Once he started the mating, for every full moon their woman would spend the month with each of them separately, and that would bind her to them.

"We've got a year, Tom. This is insane," Guy said.

"No, it's not insane. It's fucking time we found our woman."

If everything went to plan, Tom would start the binding ceremony that would result in all of them touching her while he was inside her. Most women would love six men completely devoted to them. He hoped the woman he picked was the right one and not just an act of desperation on his part.

****

Kitty Evans groaned and rubbed at her eyes. Memories of being stood at the bus stop and then the hot man with the sinful brown eyes approaching her, rushed through her. Opening her eyes, she jerked up in bed as six men stared at her. All the men in the room were different yet the same. Glancing at each one in turn, Kitty knew they were brothers. Licking her lips, she noticed they followed the action.

"Okay, erm, what the hell is going on?" Her shoes were missing, and she was on a bed, in a house she didn't recognize. The guy from the bus stop stepped forward. "I know you."

"I'm Tom Snow. These are my brothers, and you're our mate."

Staring at them all, Kitty burst out laughing. "Good one, and now I'm bored and need to get going." She moved toward the end of the bed ready to start travelling to wherever she wanted to go. When was the last time she'd been asleep in a comfortable bed? She couldn't help but compare the bed she was lying on to all the others that had gone before. Having no home, no job, and no way of making a future for herself, Kitty was all alone in the world. Her mother had died from cancer a year ago. Every single penny from her childhood home had been sold to pay for the hospital bills and the funeral. Her father was a waste of time and wouldn't be helping out any time soon. Penniless, alone, Kitty had grabbed her few items of clothing and gone travelling. When she got a few waitressing jobs she saved up enough money to move on.

It wasn't a great existence, but it was one she'd come to accept.

Tom sat next to her. "No, this is not a joke. This is real life." He took hold of her hand, and she couldn't stop the thrill that charged through her from his touch. Why wasn't she terrified? Six men she didn't know and she was more turned on than afraid. It was weird and strange, and none of it made sense.

"Mate? What the hell are you talking about?" she asked.

Run, Kitty, run.

The other large man who'd been stood beside Tom cleared his throat. "Maybe you should tell her our names before you dive into *that*."

Tom growled.

"Look, you guys seem nice and all that for not doing stuff to me while I was sleeping, but I really don't know what you're on and you're making me very uncomfortable."

"You're not going anywhere," Tom said.

She frowned at him. For many years she'd been living her life without anyone telling her what to do. There was no way she was going to let this gorgeous, controlling man tell her what to do. Looks were not everything.

"I'm Roy." The quiet man with the hazel hair and matching eyes spoke up. His voice was soft, and she couldn't help but shiver from the intensity of his voice.

"Hi," she said. His gaze didn't fall from her eyes. There was something hypnotic about him. She got the sense he was in control no matter what was occurring. For some strange reason Kitty felt safe in knowing that about him.

"What's your name?" he asked.

"It's Kitty."

"Really?" Tom asked, interrupting their moment. She frowned and turned her attention back to the man beside her. He'd kidnapped her, and she wasn't freaking out. What was wrong with her?

"Kitty Evans is my name, and it'll be all over the news when they hear you've taken me," she said, lying.

Tom scented the air. Out of all the men, he was the oldest, strongest, and darkest in coloring. His hair looked almost black, and there was an edge in his eyes. None of this made any sense to her at all.

"You're not claimed by another man. You're all alone in this world," Tom said, obviously seeing right through her lie.

Biting her lip she looked down at her hands, which were clasped together in her lap.

"Damn, he's going to fuck this up like he does everything." One of the men knelt in front of her. He didn't touch her but caught her eye by the charming smile on his face. "Hi, I'm Guy Snow. Forgive my alpha here. He's a bit of an ass when it comes to women. His age makes him a little impatient."

She chuckled and heard a growl come from beside her. The sound made her pussy pulse in awareness. Taking a deep breath, she closed her eyes.

Kitty gasped as she felt all of them approach and inhale. Opening her eyes, she wasn't wrong. All six men were watching her, sniffing the air around her.

"I've really woken up in a fantasy land," she said, rubbing her throbbing temple.

"No, you haven't." Tom took hold of her hands. He was so warm, and his scent surrounded her, making her feel comforted by his presence alone. She whimpered, not understanding what the hell was going on. Waiting for a bus shouldn't lead to this much confusion. "I'm Tom and you've met Roy and Guy. The guy with the glasses is Stuart. He's always got his head in a book. Then there are the twins. It's hard to tell them apart, but I can by scent. Mark and Joey."

She watched each man step forward. Kitty saw

the difference in the two twins immediately. Mark was the serious one. His arms were folded, and there was a frown on his face whereas Joey looked happy. She figured Mark could never really pull offs that happiness if his life depended on it.

Why was she even thinking about these men?

"Why did you take me? None of this makes any sense to me."

Tom stroked her cheek. She wanted to pull away, but instead she stayed seated, watching him.

"You're our woman, Kitty. I can't let you go. You're our mate."

She laughed. "You see, every time you say 'mate' I think of werewolves and vampires, which is crazy. None of them exist."

"Joey, change."

Turning toward the indicated twin, Kitty watched in rapt amazement as the man started to strip. He removed his shirt, and she covered her eyes.

Tom pulled at her hands. "Watch."

Giving Joey her full attention, she watched as slowly his body changed. Where there was once skin fur remained. Bones were broken, but she didn't hear them break. They seemed to mold into something she didn't recognize, and then she saw the wolf standing before her.

Everything went blank.

Chapter Two

Tom caught her before she hit the floor. Kitty had passed out at the sight of the wolf. Joey changed back, completely naked with a new pair of jeans shredded around him.

"Great, these cost me over fifty bucks to get," Joey said.

"How are we supposed to mate to a woman who can't even stay conscious for us?" Mark asked.

Rubbing his eyes, Tom eased her back under the covers. This was their mate. He sensed it and felt his wolf beneath the surface. His wolf scented her skin and knew the truth like him. Kitty was their woman, and no matter what his brothers said, he wasn't letting her go.

"This is our mate," he said, facing his brothers.

"Tom, she doesn't even know about our kind," Roy said.

"So? It doesn't matter. We'll make her aware of them."

"Is this because of your age?" Guy asked. "There are plenty of women in the world to fuck and mate with."

"I don't have time!" He yelled the words, glancing down at Kitty to make sure he hadn't woken her up.

Motioning for them to move out of the room, he closed the door, locking it behind him. He didn't want to risk her escaping or hurting herself in any way.

"This is insane. You can't steal a girl and expect her to mate with you just because you think you're out of time."

Tom growled, shoving Guy up against the wall. They were brothers, but he was the alpha and for that reason he demanded some respect even from them. "Don't even start trying to tell me what to do." He snarled, getting up close in Guy's personal space before he took a step back. "If all of you were to access your wolf and get a good sniff of her, you'd all realize that the woman passed out in bed is our destined mate. I didn't pick a woman out of desperation. I picked the woman meant for us."

He'd gone out hunting for a woman in desperation, but he wasn't about to tell them the truth. Desperation had been his motivation, but he'd succeeded in finding the right woman for him.

Letting out a breath, he stared at each of them in turn.

"Tom, she has to agree," Mark said.

"I know what the claiming is all about. Didn't any of you scent her interest in us? I smelled her desire, and she wants us." Tom would argue for the rest of the day if it meant convincing his brothers of his decision.

"Her body wants us. Her mind is not sure," Roy said, cutting through his argument.

"I don't care. She'd our mate, and we're going through with this. By the end of the month I'll be initiating the claiming, and from that moon for the next six we all have to bond with her." It was their mating rule as a pack and as brothers. "Please, don't try and tell me what we need as a pack. I know what we need."

He left them alone and headed downstairs out of the kitchen door and into the cold air. Tom needed the cold in order to deal with the thoughts running around his head. Nothing was safe, and he felt on edge. With every day that passed his wolf grew closer and closer to the surface, begging to be released. He knew he couldn't let his wolf come out even though the fight to stay human was harder each passing moon.

This is it. Kitty is our mate, and we'll all be fine. Everything will be fine so long as my brothers do as I bid and mate with her.

Staring up at the sky, he saw the clear blue and felt the crisp cold edge against his skin.

"I can do this."

"We won't hate you if we all turn into wolves," Roy said, invading his quiet.

Turning around, he looked at his brother. There were only a few years separating them, and there were times Roy felt more like his twin than anything else. Roy knew what he was thinking, feeling, and knew how to handle him.

"Really? What about in twenty years when we can't be around humans anymore because the scent of flesh and blood would be too hard to control?" Tom asked. It was so easy for all of his brothers to assure him of their feelings. None of them knew what it was like to live with their beast so close every day. He did. Being alpha meant he needed to be at one with his beast in order to protect and serve the pack. Unlike his brothers, he couldn't just decide to not be in charge. This was his destiny. This was the path his father had warned him about time and again.

Closing his eyes, he stared back up at the sky, which held the only calm he was interested in.

"Are you really sure?"

"The others are doubting me?" he asked.

"They're not sure if you've made the right decision or the desperate decision." Tom wouldn't get angry. They all thought he was hanging on by a thread, and none of them were wrong. He was hanging on by a thread, but he'd been doing his damn hardest not to show any of them how bad it was getting.

"Think about it, and you've got to talk with Kitty."

Tom chuckled. "I will. Can you believe we're

going to be mated to a woman named Kitty?"

"It has a nice ring to it, Kitty and the wolf." Roy laughed, leaving him alone.

Letting out a sigh, Tom wished his father was here to talk to. His situation was growing worse, and only Kitty held the key to making him better.

"Please, let me stay in control long enough for this." The full moon was close, and he was risking everything on his wolf.

Don't fail me.

Heading inside, Tom took the stairs two at a time. Opening the door, he sat in a chair, waiting for his woman to wake up. He didn't mind waiting. When she was awake he'd be here, waiting to talk to her. To do anything she needed.
****

Kitty stretched out her muscles. She'd not slept well in months, and her body suddenly felt more of her own that ever before. Glancing from side to side, she saw Tom sat down beside the bed watching her.

Sitting up, she recalled everything that happened, including Joey turning into a wolf. Holding the blanket up against her chin, she stared at the man who'd brought her into this situation.

"I can understand why you're scared, but I promise you have no reason to be," he said. There was no one else inside the room, other than him.

"Where's your brother?" she asked, shocked by the scratchy sound to her voice.

"He's doing something around the house, I'm sure. We do a lot of stuff to keep ourselves busy." He stood up and sat on the bed beside her.

Should she protest?

"Are you going to hurt me?" She looked up to see him frowning.

"No, we'd never hurt you, Kitty. You're safe with us, I promise."

Nodding, Kitty checked out the room. Without the other four men, she felt there was room to finally breathe. "Thank you. For not hurting me."

He reached over, stroking her cheek. "I'd never hurt you."

She believed his words even though he'd kidnapped her. Was this some kind of Stockholm Syndrome?

Shaking her head, she looked at him. "Why? We barely know each other, and in my experience, people always hurt each other."

"I'm not most people, baby. I'm part wolf."

What did she say after that?

Kitty couldn't deny his claim. She was living amongst wolves. "It must be nice changing and being able to run wild," she said, rubbing her arms in an attempt to warm up.

"You've got problems?" he asked. "Are there people waiting for you back home?"

"No, there's no one who cares about me." Kitty bit her lip. She'd just admitted to her kidnapper that there was no one looking for her.

You were checking him out before he came over.

She couldn't deny the feelings evoked within her when she was around him. He took claim of every part of her senses without even trying. Licking her lips, she became aware of how dry her throat was.

Within seconds Tom had a drink in hand and was offering her a sip.

"You've got good reflexes as well," she said, taking the drink and sipping from the straw.

"Look, this is a lot to take in, and if you want no part in this, I understand," he said.

Holding her hand up to stall him, Kitty took a drink. When she was finished, she handed him back the cup and stared at him. "First, why am I here?" she asked. For most of her life she'd been able to process thoughts and emotions a lot faster than other people. She'd never had time to dwell, and instead of staying down, she'd risen above all the battles she and her mom faced.

"Do you want the truth or for me to sugarcoat the reason why you're here?" he asked.

"I need the truth."

"Fine, my wolf recognizes your scent as my mate. We're a pack of brothers and are destined to share a mate. You're that woman."

"Wait, hold up, I'm supposed to mate six men?" she asked. The idea didn't put her off.

"It sounds like a lot," he said.

"It is a lot." She ran a hand down her face trying to process everything.

"You'd be the only woman," Tom said. "You wouldn't have to share us with anyone else. We'd be devoted to only you, your happiness and your pleasure."

His words shouldn't sound so tempting.

"What needs to happen?" she asked

Was she even considering this? No, there's no way she should be thinking about sticking around.

Another quick look around the spacious room, Kitty let out a sigh. If this room was anything to go by, the rest of the house would be a dream.

"This would be all yours," he said.

She glanced at him, seeing the hope shining back at her. When had she been able to read emotions so clearly?

"What needs to happen?" She asked the question again, trying to bring some focus into her world.

"I would have to start the claiming ceremony at

the full moon, making you our woman. After the full moon you will have to spend one moon month with each of my brothers until, at the end, you'd be with me. During that time you'll bond with each of my brothers and then finally with me. When you and I are mated, we'd have another mating that would cement our bond and that of the pack together."

She took a deep breath, trying to work through what he was saying.

"You make it sound so easy," she said. "It takes a long time."

"Yes, mating to each other and that of a pack has to be long to assure all that it's the right bond forming."

Kitty nodded, understanding. "You're all okay with sharing the same woman?"

"It's what we've been waiting for."

"Waiting for, seriously, you think that's romantic?" she asked.

He smiled, and then he got all serious. "I can promise you, Kitty, we will cherish every part of you. You'll be treated like a queen."

"Tom, I don't know you."

"Then stick around and give us all a chance. If, by the time the full moon is up, you can't stand the sight of us, then you can leave." His jaw tensed, and he stopped talking to look down.

"What is it?" she asked.

"Nothing, this is just important to us all. I need you to make a choice on your own." He stood up and walked to the door. "You can leave at any time. If you wish to be with us then come down for dinner." Tom continued to stare at her.

She watched him finally leave. When he was gone, she left the bed to look out of the window. The scenery was beautiful. She'd never seen anything so amazing and bright. Pulling a seat to the window she sat down and looked out at the passing day. She saw each of the men she'd met in her bedroom, doing something outside, from chopping wood, to playing ball. They found any way to keep working.

"What do you think, Mom?" she asked the room. Her mother was dead, but it didn't do her any harm to ask for a little help. "Do you think I should give them a chance?"

Nothing answered her. For the past year her life had been nothing but shit. She had little to look forward to. Six men were better than none, and all of her men were sexy and hot.

With her decision made, she left the bedroom, going downstairs. She found all of them in the kitchen surrounding a pot of stew. They stopped talking the moment they saw her.

"I'd like to stay," she said. "I'd like to give this mating thing a try."

Chapter Three

Over the next couple of days, Tom worked harder than he'd ever worked in his life to make Kitty feel at home. He'd never expected her to agree after taking her off the street. She seemed so relaxed when she was around them all. Sitting at the kitchen counter he watched her eating a bowl of cereal and looking at a magazine. Guy was sat on one side with Roy on the other. Stuart was reading a book while Joey and Mark were arguing about a movie they'd watched the night before.

For the first time since their parents died peacefulness had fallen on the room. Sipping at his coffee, he watched her twirl a strand of blonde hair around her finger. She wore one of his shirts with Roy's jeans. None of the clothes they owned fit her. He'd checked through the bag he'd brought with her and been surprised to find the barest essentials packed away.

"You keep staring at me, and you're going to make me worried," Kitty said, turning toward him.

"You're a beautiful woman," he said, taking a gulp of the hot liquid. Her cheeks heated, and her flush smelled so fucking sweet. His cock hardened in response. He'd not taken a woman in so long or had any kind of response to a female in a long time.

"She has such a sexy blush," Joey said.

Kitty went back to eating her breakfast, but he saw the slight smile on her lips. She was happy with their compliments.

"What are you doing today?" he asked, drawing her attention back to him.

"Erm, Stuart offered to take me out to explore." She looked toward Stuart who was reading a book and not paying attention. Screwing up the shopping list, Tom aimed it at his brother's head.

Stuart came out of his book with a start. "What?" he asked.

"Are you still taking me around to explore?" Kitty nibbled on her lip. Tom wanted to suck that lip in his mouth. He wanted to do a hell of a lot more to her.

"Yeah, is it that time already?" Stuart slammed the book closed and rose. "I'd rather spend time with you than in a musty old book." He dropped the book to the table and reached for her hand.

"Erm, you're ready to go?"

He nodded. "I've got a little picnic basket ready for us, so we don't have to venture back here for dinner."

Tom watched her get up and leave. Seconds later the door closed, echoing around the whole house.

"You were right," Guy said.

"About what?"

"She's the right woman for the mating." Guy got up and left the table. Tom sighed in relief.

"We're waiting to judge," Joey said, speaking for both him and Mark. Those two had a bond that Tom would never understand.

All too soon he and Roy were the only ones left.

"What are you thinking?" Tom asked.

"She's our woman. I just hope she can handle the claiming and the months to come. It takes its toll, and by the end of it she could become pregnant." Roy stopped and ran a finger over his lips. Tom watched his brother contemplate their situation. "A lot is riding on two weeks of getting to know each other. I hope you know what you're doing."

Roy stood, ready to leave.

"Wait, there's something I need your help with." He poured another coffee for himself and headed toward the office. Firing up the laptop, Tom sat down. Roy pulled up a chair, sitting beside him.

"What do you need my help with?" Roy asked.

"I want to buy Kitty some new clothes. I like seeing her in our clothes, but I think something new would be good for her."

Roy accessed the account. "Funny you should say that. I was looking at some new clothes for our woman."

"Do you think I made a mistake?" Tom asked while they were waiting for the websites to load.

"No, I don't. I enjoy her company. She's funny, but I get the sense that she's hurt about something."

Tom agreed. "Kitty's experienced loss. Hopefully over the next six moons she'll become acquainted with us, and we'll give her everything she needs."

"Who will be going first?" Roy leaned back, letting Tom look at the clothes he'd picked. He put the items he liked in the box ready to purchase them.

"I can't go first. You know I have to wait until the final moon to make the final claiming." He started the mating, and it ended with him.

"I know."

"It's between you and the others." Tom tapped on the mouse, ordering some sexy lingerie for her.

"Do you think we should put a background check on her?"

He glanced at Roy. "You think we need to run one? Your scent is not convincing enough?"

"I'm more than happy with my sense of smell. What I don't like is not knowing anything about her."

"We can't force her to open up. Everything will come clear during the mating." Tom looked toward the calendar seeing the date in just over a week was circled. He didn't have long to discuss it with Kitty.

This was his responsibility as alpha, to take the lead and bring their woman into the picture of what was required of each of them.

"She'll freak out if she's not ready," Roy said.

"How did you know I was thinking about that?"

"You were looking at the calendar. It doesn't take a genius to realize what's on your mind."

Finalizing the order Tom sat back. "I'll get her ready and make sure she's with us the whole way."

He didn't have much longer as a human. His wolf purred beneath the surface, waiting for a moment of weakness to take over. Tom waited for Roy to leave before he dropped his head in his hand. So much of their future was riding on this coming month. What would he do if this didn't work?

No, he couldn't think like that. Becoming a wolf was not an option. He'd fought for a long time, and he refused to give up now.

****

Kitty stared out at the night in the study. Most of the men had gone to bed. She'd been in bed for a long time before finally giving up on sleep and making her way downstairs. This was the one room that smelled like her men.

Her men?

Crap, when had she started to think of the Snow brothers as her men?

She couldn't even think around them. They were so attentive, and they made it hard for her to focus on what she was doing. Wrapping her arms around her waist, Kitty inhaled their scent and realized she didn't want to go. Tom, Roy, Guy, Stuart, Joey, and Mark had gotten under her skin. Each man was totally different, and she found herself falling for each of them already.

It hadn't been a week, and yet she was falling in love with them. Tom was so dominant that he grabbed her attention from simply walking into a room. She knew he was the alpha. Stuart, during their time together, explained all the finer details of the pack. Tom was alpha, with Roy as the beta and the next in command going down the line. Joey was the youngest as he was born minutes after Mark.

If she went through with the claiming she'd have all six men at her mercy. She smiled thinking about having all of their hands and gazes on her body. Kitty wasn't a small woman, not at all. She had curves, and she loved food, always had and always would.

Shaking, she closed her eyes thinking about what it would feel like to have all six men caressing her, stroking between her thighs or against her breasts. She let out a moan, squeezing her thighs together to stem the flow of cream she felt pooling out of her cunt. Fuck, she'd not been this turned on for a long time. Her hands shook as she reached out to the window frame to hold on to.

"What's the matter, baby?" Tom asked, startling her.

Opening her eyes, she looked behind her to see the man who'd taken her from the boring world she lived in to the orgasms and love he promised were in her future. Taking a deep breath, she kept her gaze on him at all times. He walked further into the room.

"You know I can smell you, don't you, baby?"

"Smell me?"

"Yeah, I can scent that sweet cunt of yours flowing. You're killing me with need, Kitty. I want to be a kitten to you and lick you until you scream against my mouth."

Her nipples tightened at his words.

Within seconds his hands were on her hips pulling her closer toward him. She didn't resist him. Kitty wasn't afraid of the man in front of her. He'd shown her more kindness than she ever expected from him.

This was like a fairy tale story where she'd been taken by a beast but fallen in love with him at the same time. There was more to Tom than the domineering alpha. He was sweet and always took care of her. In his arms, she felt cherished.

His hands moved down to her ass, cupping her cheeks tightly.

"Stop getting turned on," he said, growling against her ear.

The noise had her gasping, holding onto his arms tightly while he nuzzled her neck.

She moaned as his teeth bit down, not enough to draw blood but enough for her to know he meant business. Her pussy was on fire with need.

"Tom," she said, gasping.

"Stop driving me crazy. I've only got so much control."

"Give up your control." She leaned back to look in his eyes.

"What?"

"You heard me. Give up your control. I want you, Tom. I want this. Please, mate with me and make me part of your pack. It's what I want." Her outburst was the complete truth. No matter how many times she tried to deal with logic, nothing was logical about this situation. She was living with werewolves, the kind that turned all furry and growly at the full moon.

"You're sure?"

"This is the only thing in my life I've ever been sure of. I know what I want, Tom."

He cupped her cheek, stroking the backs of his fingers across her lips. "Once I start this at the full moon there will be no going back. You can't fight this, and you'll be with all six of us for the rest of your life."

She took hold of his hand and brought it to his lips. Pressing her nose against his wrist she took a deep inhale. Her body came alive under his scent. There was something calming and yet sexy about his smell alone.

"Fuck, you really do want this."

"I've got no one. There's no one looking for me or wanting me. What you and your brothers are offering is a dream come true." She let him go to run fingers through her hair. During the last week she'd not been open with any of them. Each of the men had given her a part of themselves while she kept herself at bay. "What I have in my backpack, that's all I own. My mother died of cancer a year ago. I had to sell everything to pay for her hospital bills then her funeral."

"What about your father?"

"He was a waste of space and caused more damage than he could ever repair." She glanced down at his chest unable to meet his gaze.

"Is this why you've given yourself to us?" Tom asked.

She bit her lip. "Partly. I've been alone for a long time. I mean, it's crazy right, but none of you scare me at all. The thought of being with you all excites me. I'm not terrified when I'm around you." She pressed little circles into his shirt as she spoke. "You must think I'm crazy for agreeing to this."

"I don't think you're crazy for agreeing, Kitty. I want to make sure you want this and don't feel pressured into doing something you'll regret."

"You mean being kidnapped wasn't being pressured?" she asked, looking up and smiling.

"I didn't act right. I shouldn't have taken you against your will." He stroked her cheek.

"I know, but I don't regret what you did, Tom. If

you hadn't have taken me when you did, I'd still be travelling from place to place not finding anywhere to settle down. I'm being a little selfish. I was abandoned by my own father when the going got tough. With six men, there's no risk of being left alone."

"Hey, don't you ever worry about him again. He'll never hurt you or be part of your life. We'll take care of you."

Before she could say anything, his lips were covering hers. She moaned, opening up beneath him. Tom made her feel so special when she was in his company. Touching his arm, she tried to get closer, but he kept her away from him. Kitty fought to get close to him.

Tom kept her at arm's length.

"Why?" she asked, pulling away.

His eyes were dark with a hint of amber. A growl erupted out of his throat. The sound turned her on, and she couldn't help but lick her lips, trying to taste him on her mouth.

"You're a fucking menace," he said.

"Please, Tom, I want this. I'm ready."

"I can't." The words came out through gritted teeth.

"He can't claim you until the full moon," Roy said. She looked over Tom's shoulder to see all the men looking at her. The heat in their eyes couldn't be mistaken for anything other than pure sex.

"If you're sure we'll be more than happy to mate with you," Guy said, smiling at her.

"Yes, I'm sure. If you all want me then I'd be more than happy to be with you all."

Each man nodded. Even Mark nodded, which surprised her. Out of all of the brothers he was the one who didn't voice or show any desire for her.

THE PACK CLAIMS A MATE

The full moon couldn't come fast enough. She hoped she was ready for what they all had in store. The next few months were going to be the longest of her life.

Chapter Four

The Claiming

Tom stared up at the full moon. He was stood outside in his backyard looking up at the moon, wearing a bathrobe so he wouldn't scare Kitty. There was nothing else for him to do other than wait for Kitty to come to him. His other five brothers were standing in the same style bathrobe, talking and waiting.

He'd removed his watch in order to stop himself glancing down at the time. It didn't matter what time he started the claiming, only that he started it this night. Once the sun rose then he was in trouble. He'd have to wait another month before he started the claiming. Stupid werewolf rules.

"She'll come," Roy said.

"Have you decided who is going to start the first month?" Tom asked, trying to distract himself.

"You'll wait and see." Roy left his side and started to walk away. Tom reached out to stop him. "What?"

Taking a deep breath, Tom tried to get himself together before he asked his question. "Do you think I acted rashly?" It was the first time he'd ever doubted his decision.

Roy chuckled. "You're doubting yourself now when we've got moments before Kitty comes to us?"

"This is important to me. Bringing Kitty home is different from mating with her."

Roy took a step closer and put a hand on his shoulder.

"You're the alpha. You've got senses none of us are ever going to understand. I did think you acted rashly at first, but the more time I spend with Kitty, I see what you see. Your wolf is an amazing judge of character."

Roy smiled. "I hope she is our future. There is no other person I'd rather be with."

While Roy walked away, Tom took his time to look at his brothers. Joey and Mark were arguing over something while Guy was typing on his phone. He was probably playing on one of those internet games that he loved so much.

Rolling his eyes, Tom saw Stuart was reading a book again. When would his brother ever get out of a book? He'd have to warn Stuart about what was expected of him at the full moon when it was his turn.

Suddenly quiet settled over them all. He saw they were all looking over his shoulder. Tom turned and froze as the beauty headed toward them startled him. Kitty wore a sheer white nightgown. The fabric didn't cover her body at all, yet it covered enough to make him wish for it to disappear.

His cock hardened at the sight. Tom wanted to rid himself of their clothing and feast upon her body.

She walked toward him. Her hair was bound above her head, the golden locks cascading down her body. He loved her hair. It was so silken to the touch.

The scent of her nerves came to him. Stepping closer he closed the distance between them.

"You're nervous."

"Can you blame me? Six men surround me, and not once have you seen me naked." She rubbed her hands down her thighs, nibbling her lip. Kitty didn't look away from him. Her blue eyes sparkled in the moon light.

Reaching toward her, he lifted her face to the moon. "We'll all be touching you this night, but I'll be the only one doing the claiming," he said.

She nodded, letting out a breath. "Okay, I'm ready."

Taking her hand, he led her toward his brothers.

When they were near them, he let her go allowing his brothers to move closer. Mark got to her first. Tom watched his brother band an arm around her waist and pull her close.

"I didn't think you liked me," Kitty said. Her voice sounded incredulous.

"I was never going to get attached to a woman who wasn't sticking around," Mark said. Seconds later, Tom watched as Mark kissed her. The kiss wasn't gentle but a possession of lips. His young brother really did want Kitty.

Smiling, he saw the approval in the rest of his brothers.

"I never get my hopes up to have them dashed away." Mark stroked her nose and face with his finger. "When it's our moon I'll treat you like a goddess. You'll have no doubt about my feelings. I promise you."

Tom had no doubt about Mark's feelings, and he was thankful to know that all of his brothers wanted this before he finally claimed her.

Next, Joey came forward. This was part of their ceremony. Each of his brothers had to accept her within their fold.

"On our moon I'll give you everything your heart desires. There will be nothing you want as I'll give you all." Joey brushed his lips against hers. He leaned forward to whisper in her ear. If it wasn't for Tom's good hearing he wouldn't have a clue what Joey whispered. "Distance makes the heart grow fonder, and by the time you're with me, I'll have you screaming my name."

Kitty gasped but couldn't say anything as Joey moved away. Guy simply kissed her deeply, stroking her body before moving away.

Roy moved forward and held her close, stroking

up and down her body. With each passing minute, Kitty relaxed, and she'd be ready for them.

Stuart finally approached. Tom was shocked to see his brother without a book in his hands.

"I'll worship you, Kitty." Stuart got to his knees before her. "You'll never be afraid in this world again." He kissed her hand and stepped back.

It was time for Tom. He moved closer. She turned to him with a smile on her face.

"Is it time for me to be your woman?"

"Yes."

She nodded. "I'm ready. I'm more than ready to become your woman."

He wrapped an arm around her waist and spun her to face his brothers. Pushing some of her hair off her face, he kissed her neck.

"Tom?" The nerves were back.

"Baby, look at each of them. They're watching you, hoping to wait their turn in claiming you." Stroking a hand down her hip, he settled his hand on her stomach, caressing the rounded curves. "Do you see the lust in their eyes?"

"Yes," she said, sighing.

"Never be afraid of what we can give you. I love you, Kitty," he said, voicing his feelings.

Her head jerked toward him. "Do you lie?"

"No, I'd never lie to you." He kissed her cheek. "Are you ready to become our mate?"

"Yes, please, Tom, make me your mate."

****

Kitty moaned as his lips brushed her cheek. All the men were watching her as Tom touched her. Closing her eyes, she allowed the feeling to settle over her. The nerves that had been inside her when approaching her men had slowly disappeared. No one could mistake the want in their eyes. They all wanted her, and it made her feel so happy. She didn't know it was possible to be wanted by six men.

"I'm going to make you my mate. I'm going to touch your body and have you screaming in pleasure, and then we're never letting you go, baby. Would you like that?"

"Yes." She screamed the words for all of them to hear.

His hands moved up to the top of her gown. She'd found the gown waiting for her on her bed after she'd taken a bath. This very gown was the reason she'd taken so long to come out. How could anyone leave the house with nothing to cover their nakedness?

That was all about to change as Tom released her nightgown, button by button.

Taking a deep breath, she opened her eyes, wondering what she'd see. His five brothers were watching her, but she didn't see revulsion. She saw desire, lust, and a burning need.

"I think our woman needs to see your reactions to her body," Tom said. He'd released the top part of the gown and pushed it off her shoulders.

One by one, his brothers removed their robes, and she saw exactly what their response was to her body. Each of them was rock hard. Guy gripped his flesh first, fisting the tip. Roy stared at her with a lazy curiosity.

Licking her lips, she stared at him wondering what he was thinking about.

"They all want you."

She could see that. Their gazes were focused on her as her tits were revealed to them. The cool air should have affected her. It didn't. She felt hot, consumed by a burning fire that only each of her men could put out the flames.

"I smell your cream. You're getting wetter for me."

"Please, Tom, don't keep me waiting too long."
He pushed her gown to the floor. She stepped out of it.
He pulled her back against his body so she was still staring out at the brothers.

"Isn't she a thing of beauty?" Tom asked.

"Her scent is driving me crazy. I feel my wolf is close," Roy said.

"She's so fucking beautiful." Guy growled the words at her.

Each of them growled at her. The lust was clear to see on their faces. Tom was naked, pressing himself against her back. She whimpered at the feel of his thick cock pressing against her back.

"Do you want this, baby?"

"Yes, mate me, Tom." She'd taken to begging, and she wasn't used to begging to get what she wanted.

"I'll give you everything you ever wanted, and my brothers will watch. They'll be part of the claiming."

"Will they be fucking me, too?" she asked.

She heard several male moans surround them.

"No, they won't fuck you today. You'll get your chance with each of them and me. I'm the alpha, and I'm the only one who can claim you." Tom took her down to the ground. She looked up at him with the moon shining behind his back. The sight before her took her breath away.

"It's time, Kitty."

His words soothed her.

"Thank you for giving me this second chance."
She didn't know what he meant by that, but she was happy to be part of their world. There was nothing she wanted more than to be their mate.

He leaned down brushing his lips against hers.

The touch started out sweet, and when she opened her lips to make the kiss deeper, Tom took full advantage.

She felt his hands all over her body, stroking and caressing but never actually touching her intimately. He was making it hard for her to want to do anything other than to attack him so he'd fuck her.

Tom released her lips and kissed down her neck. He nibbled on her flesh before going down to the tops of her breasts. She cried out as his tongue circled the nubs and then bit down. He didn't draw blood. The pleasure combined with the sharp bite of pain made her writhe underneath him.

"You're so wet."

She felt her cream leaking out of her cunt and dripping down to her anus.

His fingers caressed up her inner thigh then landed onto her pussy. She stared into his eyes, unable to look away from him.

He groaned. "She's so wet."

A finger slid between her slit, stroking up then down. He circled her clit then moved down to thrust two fingers inside her. Two fingers were deep inside her, coated with her cream. Tom kissed his way down her body. His tongue dipped into her belly button. Her breathing went from steady to erratic as he stared at her from between her thighs.

Tom opened her sex with his fingers and started to tongue her clit. She cried out, sinking her fingers into the grass to grip at something. Her hands were removed from the grass, and she saw Roy holding one hand as Guy held the other.

Stuart stroked her hair while the twins caressed her thighs.

Whimpering, she watched all of them as they devoted their time to her pleasure.

The alpha's tongue plunged inside her.

She screamed, and Stuart claimed her lips swallowing her sounds.

Hands stroked over her body, and all their touches were driving her closer and closer to orgasm.

"Please, don't stop," she said, begging them.

Kitty had never once felt like this. Every part of her body felt like it was burning alive. Her skin was a mass of pure sensation that only her men could deal with.

"You're our woman," Roy said. "Your pleasure is our pleasure."

They all murmured.

"Come for me, baby," Tom said, stroking three fingers inside her cunt. His tongue caressed over her clit.

Her orgasm consumed her, crashing over her wave after wave. All of her men held her through the pleasure.

Through the slits of her eyes she watched as Joey took over caressing her clit for Tom to grip his cock.

Now it was time, and she couldn't wait to start.

Chapter Five

Tom fisted his cock watching her cream escape her cunt. His hands were shaking. This was the moment he thought would never come. Closing his eyes, he sent up a prayer to whoever was looking over him this month. Kitty was everything to him and his family. She'd be the mother of their children and the person to stabilize his family.

Stroking his cock against her entrance, he took the time to look at all of his brothers. They were waiting, and the anticipation on their faces was alive within him. His wolf was close to the surface, loving the feel of their mate. Kitty was destined to be theirs, and her smell was amazing.

Joey removed his hands from her pussy, and his brothers simply touched her skin as he plunged into her heat.

Kitty screamed, and he held her down with his brothers. "Kitty Evans, my mate, my life." Tom stopped to pull out of her heat. He stared into her eyes, feeling the power of the full moon on his back. "I take you as my mate. I claim you before the full moon in front of my brothers and all that is natural. The earth accepts you as do I."

His brothers answered to the call, accepting Kitty as their woman.

Tom pounded inside her, feeling her tight heat surrounding him.

"Kitty, do you take us into your body and accept the claiming for the moons to come?"

He stayed still within her waiting for her to respond. This was the hardest thing he'd ever done in his life. Her smell was so pure and fresh even though she wasn't a virgin. The tight heat of her cunt was so welcoming, and he didn't want to stop or to leave.

"Yes, I accept you, Tom Snow, and your brothers. I'll love you with all my heart, body, and soul."

"It's time, Tom," Roy said.

Changing positions, Tom stayed inside her warmth and had her straddling his lap.

"I bind you to me and to my pack, Kitty." He exposed her neck and bit down with the fangs of his wolf. The alpha inside him roared to life, accepting her blood into his body. His fangs sank his wolf saliva into her body, mating her to him and to the pack.

She cried out, pulling on his hair as he pumped into her body.

Tom felt her second orgasm and tightened his hold on her hips as his own orgasm crashed over him. He pumped his seed into her tight warmth, growling as the mating was complete.

The connection running between them was alive and had his body pulsing all over. He'd done it. He'd finally mated with his woman.

"Yes, Tom, yes," she said, whimpering.

"I've got you, baby." He stroked her back and nodded for Roy to come close. His brother licked at her neck and pierced the flesh once again.

Each of his pack needed to taste her blood and add their saliva to initiate the claiming. After Roy, Guy came, then Stuart, until the twins took their turn one by one.

"The mating has begun."

Pulling out of her tight heat, Tom lifted her up in his arms. "What happens now?" Kitty asked.

"I give you to my brother." He passed her to Roy. "The month is yours. Mate her, claim her, and bring her back to us in one piece."

Staring into Kitty's eyes, Tom turned on his heel

and walked away. This was the hardest thing he'd ever done, but as alpha this was his task to complete. Closing his eyes, he went toward the forest. The wolf took over as he turned into his monster.

He'd started the claiming, and now he couldn't even touch her until it was his turn. Each of his brothers would get their chance before him. For the first time in his life, Tom was jealous of his brothers.

Turning back into his human form when he was far enough away, he looked up at the moon.

Minutes passed before he felt the rest of his brothers, his pack behind him.

"Roy has taken her to the house at the bottom of the lake. We are not allowed to approach until the next moon, and only then will Guy be allowed near her," Stuart said.

Tom nodded, feeling the tears close to the surface.

"You did the right thing," Joey said, sounding serious for once.

"I did the right thing? I hate these rules. I shouldn't be able to walk away," Tom said.

"These are our rules, brother," Guy said. "We have to follow the rules or risk being a wolf forever."

He knew the rules better than any of them. What he'd done was instill the insecurity, and now they all had to win Kitty back to their side. A part of himself felt torn from his chest at the distance.

"We'll get through this, and we'll help you," Mark said.

"She's our only hope. I pray that she can forgive me for walking away." He looked at the moon, wishing he wasn't cursed the way he was.

"Roy will explain everything to her. You've got nothing to fear."

Tom didn't say anything more. His job as alpha was to secure his mate. He did that, and now it was his curse to wait his turn to claim her.

As the hours passed, he felt each of his brothers leave his side. The sun was rising and the moon disappearing.

When he was alone once more, he stared at the same spot where the moon had once stood.

"No, I can't stand here not knowing what was happening." Turning back into his wolf form, he charged toward the house that had been built centuries ago for the claiming. Part of him was fighting with the other part of himself. Tom felt divided into two. There was no real part of him, other than the pain of his situation.

Tears ran down his face even as a wolf. When he saw the house, he turned back into human form. Hiding behind a tree, he closed his eyes and concentrated on listening to what was going on.

"Let me hold you," Roy said.

"No, he turned his back on me after he'd fucked me." Kitty sounded angry.

Swallowing past the lump in his throat, he moved closer.

"I'm going to explain his strange actions to you if you'll give me the chance." Something crashed followed by Roy's curse.

"No, this was a bad mistake. I'm never going to be your mate. This was a mistake. I'm not going to accept him or you again." He heard her sobs, but the scent coming from the house signified her lies. Kitty was hurt, but she wasn't walking away, or at least he hoped not.

Tom walked away from the house. This was what he feared would happen. The stupid rules were in place for him to walk away. The belief was that the female would become a stronger mate by growing closer to all of them. He had to be the last guy to mate with her in order to seal the bond rather than break it.

"You shouldn't be here," Roy said, alerting him to his brother's presence.

"I couldn't walk away."

"I don't care. This is my time with our mate. I'll fix everything and so will our brothers. This is not your battle anymore." Roy's arms were folded, blocking the view of the house as he stood beside Tom.

"Maybe if I can talk to her?"

Roy shook his head. "The claiming has happened. Now it's my turn to mate her. Back away, Tom, my alpha, and trust me to make this right. She doesn't understand our ways, and she's human. Humans are not all used to men fucking them and walking away. Give me my time with her."

He stared at his brother and knew Roy spoke the truth. If anyone could get Kitty to listen to reason, he was the man.

Tom walked away with a little spark in his heart. He'd started the claiming, and now it was up to his brothers to begin the mating.
****

Roy watched his brother go and moved back into the house. Kitty was sitting on the sofa watching television. The next month was all his. Her scent calmed his beast.

He wouldn't fail his brothers. Looking out of the front door, he saw Tom walking away. This was his brothers', and his, last chance to remain human or be cursed to be a wolf forever. Closing the door, he walked toward Kitty, sat in front of her and took the remote out of her hand.

"We're cursed beings, Kitty. You're our last

chance in more ways than you can believe. Tom is in love with you. My brothers are in love with you, and so am I. You've lost your family. Please, help me to keep mine safe," he said.

She stared at him.

"Will you help me?" he asked.

"Yes, I'll help you."

Nodding, Roy took her hand within his. The Claiming was over, and now it was time for the mating.

The End

SAM CRESCENT

THE FIRST MOON

The Pack Claims a Mate, 2

Sam Crescent

Copyright © 2014

Chapter One

Roy Snow walked beside his pack's chosen mate wishing there was something more he could say. This was the first time he'd ever been part of a claiming, and Kitty, their mate, was not helping matters. His brother and alpha had fucked up big by taking her then walking away. Roy knew his brother hadn't had a choice. Their traditions were fucked up, but they had to live by them. Tom had no choice but to walk away so that the rest of them in the pack could bond with her. It was a lame-ass rule, but other packs during a claiming had failed for not following the rules. The Snow clan didn't have a choice. Tom didn't have long left until the change took him over.

Now, Roy was the one who had to make it up to her for Tom's necessary actions, and his month was going by with him trying to make her see reason. They hadn't bonded during their time so far.

"I know it's stupid. I've not even known you all that long, and yet I thought Tom was a good man. I never thought he'd be the kind of guy to do something like that," she said. Her hands were going all over the place with her emphasis. The scents of disappointment, anger, arousal, and even need wafted to his nostrils. For two weeks he'd been listening to her vent about his brother. The constant stream of disappointment was starting to piss him off. He was starting to wonder why they were even bothering with her, but then he'd smell her, and in his heart, he knew why.

He was tired of hearing Tom's name. His brother didn't help to inspire seduction. The moment Tom's name came out of her lips, Roy's dick went flaccid. Kitty was so damn upset, and he wished there was something he could say to make her see reason or even just to shut her up.

They moved around the trees, and he hoped to God his brothers were nowhere to be seen. The other day he'd scented Mark and Joey, the twins, close by. None of them were allowed near Kitty until she'd bonded with him.

Thinking back over the last two weeks, Roy realized every time he'd tried to woo her, Kitty had pushed him away. She was keeping him at arms' length, refusing to give him chance to get to know her. Roy was known for his patience, but with two weeks already gone, he only had a limited time, and if he failed, then the whole pack failed. Every brother had to play their part in the game of the claiming.

"I mean, why not take me back to the world of the living human people? I'm no good here at all."

His temper spiked. "We're living, breathing people, Kitty."

"You're werewolves."

"It doesn't mean we're not people." He reached out, grabbing her hand, careful not to jolt her body too hard. Being a wolf gave him a lot of strength, and it would be all too easy to tear her apart. "Feel that." Her palm covered his chest. "Hard, warm, and beating. My heart beats, and I feel just like you. All of my brothers feel just like humans do. We're not immune to pain, love, loss, desire. My brother didn't walk away because he wanted to but because he had to." Roy gritted his teeth to stop from telling her the truth.

"I'm…" She stopped talking, biting into her lip. "I'm sorry."

"You better be sorry. Tom risked a great deal doing what he did, but there was a purpose in it. There's always a purpose for everything." He glanced down at the hand covering his chest. The need to take her took over. The beast within him rose. Kitty was their final chance to become free. His brothers needed him to do this. Otherwise they would be lost to the animal that claimed half of their soul.

Sinking his fingers into her hair, he fisted the length, pulling her head back to expose her neck. He saw the beating of the pulse at the base of her neck. Licking her throat, he watched her gasp.

"Now, you've wasted over two weeks of complaining about Tom. I love my brother. I love all of my brothers, but you agreed to this." He felt his cock tighten, remembering the way she had given herself to Tom at the last full moon. Her full body had been on display, and all he wanted to do was fuck her.

"I didn't agree to being used," she said, glaring at him.

He smelled the heat rising off her pussy. She was begging for a nice hard cock to satisfy her.

"You were not used. We asked you if you wanted this." He caressed her lips, knowing he was only seconds away from claiming the plump flesh. "We've got two weeks, baby. Are you doing to give me the chance to prove to you that you can love me as much as Tom?"

"When it's all over, will you walk away, too?"

"I can't answer that." Roy stared into her eyes so she saw that he would. What he couldn't say in words was easy to say with the right pointed look. She had to bond with all of the pack for this to work. They were brothers, bound by pack blood.

She let out a frustrated sigh. "I don't know if I can survive this. It hurts when you fuck me and walk away."

"You're about to have six men who will devote the rest of their lives to you. I promise you, Kitty, we don't walk away lightly. It hurts us in a different way, but it still fucking hurts." He meant that. Roy knew Tom had been torn up inside, walking away from her sweet, delightful pussy.

Leaning ever closer, he scented her desire, and his cock thickened even more.

Her hands grabbed his arms. "I don't know if I'll ever survive this," she said, whimpering.

"Not only will you survive us, you'll come to crave us, our need, our touch, our cocks. There is never going to be a day where you don't feel worshiped or cherished. We're going to love you like a wife is supposed to be loved." He kept her pressed up a tree and thanked the Lord above for the silence it brought. If he had to listen to Tom's name again he was going to go insane.

Releasing a growl, he pressed his nose against her hair and inhaled her scent. Fuck, she truly was the best woman for them. Her scent alone was worth listening to her nag.

"Roy." She spoke his name with a moan to her lips.

"I know, baby. I know." Pressing his thick cock

against her stomach, he moved his lips up to hover just over her mouth. "Give yourself to us, Kitty. Give yourself to me, and you'll want for nothing."
****

Would it really hurt to give in? Kitty felt his breath across her lips, and she wanted him in that instant. It was a desire that was going to get her in so much trouble. He could easily use her and spit her out as if she meant nothing to him.

Just like Tom.

Stop that, he didn't use you. You're going to see him again.

So many thoughts ran through her head as she glanced up at Roy. He really was a tall man. His muscles were so thick that he made her feel utterly small. Kitty smiled. She couldn't recall a time apart from being with the Snow men when she had ever felt small, delicate even.

Out of all of the brothers, Roy was the quiet, caring one. It had been easy to think about Tom's desertion when Roy was happy to remain silent and simply look at her. With Roy's gaze focused on her, she couldn't think of anything else. But then her thoughts would return to Tom and what he did, and the pain would start back up. The silence was never good for her thoughts. She always thought about the negative rather than the positive.

"What do you want, Kitty?" he asked.

His breath fanned her face, and she scented the mint he liked to suck on throughout the day. She discovered his need for mints. He told her he possessed a sweet tooth, and the mints stopped it as the strong ones hurt his tongue. It was strange the kind of conversation they had actually had together.

Strange.

Staring into his hazel eyes she felt an answering pulse deep in her core. What did she want?

Like most women she wanted to be loved, desired, and to feel sexy as if their men couldn't tear their gazes away from her. There was so much she wanted and yet could possess so little.

"I want your lips on me," she said, flexing her fingers around his arm.

Roy closed the distance between them, and then his lips were on hers. Crying out, she closed her eyes as electricity seemed to sizzle in the air between them. He knew what to do with his lips to have her begging, melting for him.

He moved his hands from her hair to cup her face, tilting her head back. The heat from his touch made her burn for him. Gasping, she pulled away to look up at him.

The hard length of his cock pressed to her stomach, making her very much aware of how happy he was to be against her.

"I'm going to lift you up now," he said.

"What?"

Hands left her face, and she felt him cup her underneath her bum. Holding onto his arms, tightly, she felt the ground leave beneath her feet as he pinned her against the hard length of the tree. Gasping for breath she continued to stare in his eyes.

Wrapping her legs around his waist she felt the heat of him through her own jeans. His cock was so long and thick that he took her breath away.

"Do you feel that? I want you so badly. For the last two weeks all I've heard is Tom's name on those precious lips. I don't want to hear his name anymore. I want to hear my name when you cry out for pleasure. I need to know you want to be here with me as much as I want to be with you," he said, scenting her skin.

Her nipples budded against the onslaught of pleasure.

"Roy," she said, whispering his name.

"Yes, I want my name on your lips. Give me a chance, Kitty. Please."

She bit her lip, staring into his eyes and knew she was completely lost forever. Why was she fighting him? What did she hope to gain by keeping herself back from him? Nothing.

Give in.

"All my brothers will fall for you. They want you to be happy."

"No," she said, pressing her finger against his lips. "If you want me to do this then you've got to stop talking about them. I've wasted two weeks of complaining about your oldest brother. Don't let me waste another moment complaining about anything else." She leaned forward to press her lips against his. They were firm to the touch. If Roy took her mind away from the pain, she wouldn't start thinking about Tom and what he did.

The scent of the forests invaded her senses as she looked at him. Her heart thumped against her chest. This was the life she'd chosen. Each of the Snow brothers was to be given a chance to mate with her, to be what she needed.

Kitty needed to realize she wasn't in the city anymore. The dating rules no longer apply. They were werewolves for fuck's sake.

"We've got two weeks left, Kitty. Give me those two weeks."

"I've wasted so much time."

He shook his head. "Then don't let us waste another moment." Roy took possession of her lips.

Melting against his touch, she circled his neck as one of his hands caressed up her body to hold onto her breast.

Crying out, she flung her head back as he kissed down her body. He tugged on the shirt she wore, exposing her breasts.

"Such beautiful tits," he said.

In one quick tug, he tore at the shirt and bra she wore, leaving her naked. The fresh air breezed over her skin making it a heady experience.

"Let me take you back to the cabin," he said.

She shook her head. "No, I don't want to go to the cabin." Crying out, she felt the heat spiraling in her pussy. "Fuck me here, now, against this tree." She tugged on his hair and slammed her lips down on his.

He placed her on the floor, and she watched him remove his clothes. His actions were smooth in comparison to hers. Kitty removed her jeans, wriggling out of them. Before she kicked them away, Roy tore them in two.

"You were not going fast enough."

Kitty knew she would never deny him again.

****

Tom smelled her arousal all the way up the forest.

"He's doing the best he can," Guy said, trying to reason with him. He was surrounded by his brothers trying to offer him support.

"She hates me. Her hatred has cost Roy two weeks." Tom ran a hand down his face. Every day was getting harder. His dreams were consumed with that of his wolf. Once the change happened there would be no going back, and his brothers would follow him into hell.

"He'll get her back. We've got no choice. We have to make this work," Mark said. "It was you that kept your fear and the truth of the change away from him. We're all in danger, and it's this chance or none at all."

The guilt claimed him. Last night he'd been so close to the change that his brothers held him down, reasoning with him. Once the change stopped he told them the truth that only Roy knew. This was their last chance with a woman. If they didn't all mate with her, they were royally fucked.

"Roy, please."

Listening to her cries, Tom hoped she gave them all a chance as she was their only one.

Chapter Two

Roy growled as the scent of her pussy wafted up to him. She was so fucking beautiful. He didn't know whether to sink to his knees and lick up her sweet cum or to ram his dick straight into her.

Tasting her cream on his tongue won. Sinking to his knees, he opened her thighs wide.

"What are you doing?" she asked, crying out.

"I'm going to lick this sweet pussy, and then I'm going to fuck you."

With the smell of her arousal and the forest surrounding them Roy felt the joy swamp him. Having the two things around him that he loved so much was intoxicating.

"You're going to give me this, aren't you, Kitty?"

"Yes." She said the word on a cry.

Feeling lust hit him, he ran his hands up her thighs until he cupped her pussy. Her heat drenched his hand, and he groaned. "You're so wet for me, baby."

"Please," she said.

"Tell me what you need."

"I need your mouth on my clit. Suck me, please."

Even without the sunlight he'd be able to see her as he had excellent eyesight. Her arousal coated her lips, and he opened them to see the jewel of her clit glinting at him. His mouth watered, and Roy couldn't wait any longer.

He sucked her clit into his mouth and felt her legs give out. Roy grabbed her hips, holding her up as he attacked her pussy. Sliding his tongue over the nub, he glided down to press inside her tight heat. Her cum was musky, beautiful, and he loved it.

"Roy," she said, crying out.

"Come on, baby. Give me your cum."

She screamed out, and he licked and sucked at her pussy. Her cream soaked his fingers as he pressed them deep inside her. Kitty took three of his fingers without difficulty.

"Please." She begged him to give her what she needed.

Only when she reached her orgasm did he get to his feet. Fisting his cock, he coated his pre-cum around the tip, groaning at the feel.

"I'm going to fuck you so good," he said. Picking her up in his arms, he waited for her to circle his hips.

He glided the tip up and down her slit, coating himself with her cum. Placing the tip at her entrance, he pressed forward, groaning as she took every inch of him.

"You're so big."

Roy smiled, looking up into her eyes. "Kiss me, beautiful."

She took his lips and groaned. He had her cum all over his mouth. Plunging his tongue into her mouth, he deepened the kiss as he fucked to the hilt inside her body. The tree was to her back, and he made sure not to hurt her.

"Fuck me, Roy, make it hurt," she said, moaning.

Taking her to the ground with the scent of the earth and grass surrounding them, he watched her tits bounce as he thrust inside her body.

He sensed his brothers were close, but he drowned out their scents and the noise they were making. There was no way he could listen to them and give Kitty what they both needed.

"Do you feel me, baby?" he asked.

"Yes, please, Roy."

Pounding inside her body, he glanced down to watch his cock disappear within her body. It was so beautiful. He could claim her right now, but it wouldn't be as effective until the night of the full moon. Hating what he would have to do, he slammed his lips down on hers and made love to her body, trying to pour his feelings into the actions.

She deserved flowers, chocolates, and a lot more time than this. One month each was all they had. The twins, they only got a month between them as they were bound by the same genes.

"I love you, Kitty," he said, speaking of his feelings. She shook her head, cupped his cheek and pressed her lips to his. Roy knew she was silencing him, stopping him from saying anything more. Kitty wasn't ready to give him the words. She was holding herself back.

Loving her body was the only way to do it.

Pumping into her body, he felt her cunt ripple in response.

"Fuck, baby, I'm going to come."

She thrust up to meet his every stroke, but something was different. Crying out, he tensed as his orgasm took him by surprise. He filled her with his cum, but he knew she was no longer in the moment. Kitty had reached orgasm, but she'd withdrawn from him as quickly.

Holding himself away from her, he stared at the ground, wondering what the fuck had happened. He was usually much better at making out a woman's emotions. Out of all of his brothers, he understood women most.

"Kitty, are you with me?" he asked, looking into her eyes.

Her nod was all he got. She didn't say anything more, and he felt like an asshole. Pulling out of her body, he picked her up and carried her back to the cabin. Once they were in the cabin he placed her on her feet. Kitty withdrew heading toward her room. He watched her go knowing he'd hurt her some way.

Stepping out of the cabin he made his way, naked, toward his brothers. "What are you doing out here?"

Tom stepped from around a tree while his other brothers made an appearance. As usual the twins, Mark and Joey, stood together.

"We wanted to make sure everything is okay," Tom said.

"No, it's not okay. She doesn't know what to do. I can feel her need, and yet she holds herself back. You all need to back off so I can gain her trust." Roy glanced at all of them in turn so they would understand his desperation. "Do you want me to fail come the full moon? You saw what just happened. If she fights me then I can't lay claim to her as well."

Roy ran fingers through his hair, the worry and fear finally getting to him. He didn't want to remain a wolf forever. This claiming required all of them.

"We'll back off," Tom said.

The others agreed and walked away. He watched them go, knowing they were as scared as he was about what was to come.

****

Lying in bed, Kitty didn't know why she was crying. She heard Roy leave the cabin after he left her alone. Why did he leave? Tucking the blanket around her body, she stared at the far wall hoping for some kind of sign for her to know what the hell was going on.

She wiped the tears from her face but didn't feel any better.

What is wrong with me?

No answer came, and she felt all over the place with her emotions. She jumped when she heard the front door slam closed. Biting her lip, she closed her eyes hoping he would give her time to get her thoughts together. The door to the bedroom opened.

"Kitty?"

Keeping her eyes closed, she didn't know why she didn't want to talk to him. The blanket was pulled back, and she felt his heat at the back of her. His hand banded around her waist, and he eased right behind her.

He was naked.

"I know you're awake," he said.

Still she didn't say anything.

Roy kissed her shoulder. "I'm not going anywhere. I'll hold you while you sleep, and when you wake up I'll still be here."

She shivered from his touch as tears spilled down her cheeks.

"Please, baby, tell me why you're crying."

Kitty didn't know why she was crying. Nothing made any sense to her anymore. She was going to be mated by a pack of six brothers, and yet at that moment she felt so alone. Everything Roy did, she couldn't help but feel used. He didn't hurt her, but come the full moon, he was going to walk away, leaving her alone.

Tom had walked away, and it hurt her to see.

"Please," he said.

"I can't." She choked on the word, gasping for breath. This wasn't supposed to be hard.

"Shh, don't cry." Roy sat up, placing her in his lap. He wrapped his arms around her as she sobbed. "Tell me what's the matter."

"No. I don't want to talk."

She'd been pulled away from her life, and among all of his brothers she felt like she was about to be torn apart. Each man was going to make her fall in love with them, and after they took her, she was going to watch them walk away. How could any woman or mate survive this kind of pain? She wasn't a wolf. Were wolves able to turn off their emotions?

"Then if you don't want to talk I'll hold you and talk for the both of us."

Kitty doubted he could talk. In the last two weeks she'd spoken a hell of a lot more than he had. His touch helped to soothe her troubles even though she wanted to remember that he would walk away.

Closing her eyes, she felt the beating of his heart. It was racing, and she'd come to know it was because of his wolf blood that it beat so fast.

"I've got no idea what you're going through. I know this, and I bet all you want to do is leave, but you can't." She stayed silent as he talked. "It's a lot to take in. Not only have you learned wolves exist but now you're about to be mated by a pack. This is never going to happen again for us, Kitty. When we're mated and the claiming is complete, you will own us the way we own you."

His hand stroked her hair, pulling the strands away from her face.

"There will be no other woman. You will be the only woman in our pack. I know this is going to tear you apart as you give a part of yourself to each of us and you're going to watch us hurt you, but I promise you, when it's all over you're going to have more than your heart's desire."

What did he mean? Roy kept hinting at more, yet he wasn't allowed to say anything. Pulling out of his arms, she climbed off the bed, staring at him. She pushed some of the blonde strands out of the way as she looked at him.

"I can't do this tonight." His seed started to slide down the inside of her thigh. "I know what you're saying, but you don't know what it's like to watch him walk away. I'm sorry for spoiling the last two weeks with Tom's name. Tonight, I need to be alone. Can I have that?"

"I've given you so much time alone."

She shook her head. "No, you haven't. I want to be alone without you watching me or looking over to take care of me."

"I don't like this. We've not got long left of this full moon. I need you—" He stopped, looking down at the bed.

"You need me to fall for you. I know, I get it, but you don't need me to fall for you tonight."

"Kitty," he said her name, and she knew he was going to try to convince her to come back to him.

Shaking her head, she took a step back. "No, I want tonight to be on my own. Please, let me have tonight."

Roy let out a sigh. "Fine, I'll leave you alone tonight even though I don't like it."

She smiled and took a step away, leaving the bedroom. His heat would have been a comfort to her. Closing the door behind her, she made her way downstairs to the freezer. She took out the chocolate ice cream and found the chocolate sauce. Kitty didn't even bother with a bowl and decided to eat the ice cream from the tub.

Sitting on the sofa, she stared into the fire that was blazing and wondered what the hell she was doing. She'd stepped into an alternate universe where men shared their women and she was surrounded by wolves.

Being with the men wasn't the problem. She couldn't help but feel used. Was she their last choice of woman to pick to claim? Old insecurities were coming forward, leaving her feeling hollow.

It wasn't Roy's fault, and come the morning she

intended to be a different person. She wouldn't think about his brothers, and it would be their time together without anyone looking in.

Chapter Three

Roy woke to the smell of bacon frying. His mouth watered, and his stomach growled letting him know how hungry he actually was. Last night had been awful. For most of the night he lay in bed listening to Kitty cry or move around downstairs. When she went silent, he walked downstairs to find her sleeping on the sofa, bundled up in a blanket. He hated the sight, wanting more than anything to carry her back to his room and to put her in bed beside him.

At the last minute he stopped himself from picking her up and taking her back to bed. Two weeks were all he had left to build up some kind of trust that she wasn't actually feeling right now. He hated how upset she'd become last night, but he wasn't going to ruin her trust by being selfish.

Climbing out of bed, he took care of business in the bathroom, donned some pants and made his way downstairs. He found her in the kitchen in one of his long shirts. She was singing to a tune playing on the radio. Roy didn't recognize the artist or the song. Watching her move was a thing of beauty and something he could spend the rest of his life doing.

He stood in the doorway to the kitchen, simply watching her. The smell from her was even better than the bacon.

She twirled around, smiling. When she caught sight of him, the smile remained, which was new.

"Hey, how did you sleep?" she asked.

"I slept well. Did you?"

"Yeah, I slept good. Okay, I know we can't have the two weeks back, but I think we can start over."

"The Claiming?"

She held her hand up, stopping him. "No, no

more talk of the claiming or of the full moon. I want us to go on a date, and so I've put dinner in the oven. We're going out together today."

"Tom wouldn't like us to go to town." He folded his arms, unsure what to do or say. On the one hand he was jumping for joy, but on the other, he knew the rules, and going to town was forbidden.

"When was the last time you went on a date? You don't need a town or city to have a date." She rolled her eyes. "We're going to spend time, talking, getting to know each other. First, you're going to eat your breakfast. I made bacon, eggs, and tomatoes. Also, here is some bread. We've got pork stew in the slow cooker, and we'll enjoy that when we get back home." Kitty sat opposite him, picking up her fork.

She was like a totally different woman.

He followed her lead and started to eat. "We can go for a walk in the forest."

"Yes, the claiming is off topic, so is sex. We'll talk about each other and other interests. I'm tired of feeling like I'm on some kind of deadline. It's hard to really get to know someone when they're trying to speed everything along."

Roy watched her eat, loving the sight of her appetite. She looked so perfect, and when she smiled she lit up his whole world.

"Are you going to eat?" she asked, pointing at his plate. "Come on, it's all good. I promise. I cooked everything through."

"It's perfect." He finished eating before she did.

"If you do the dishes I'll get dressed and we can head out, if you want?" Kitty asked.

"Sure. I'd love to do that." He watched her disappear upstairs.

Getting her to walk around naked would take

some time. He did their dishes and went around the cabin putting a few things straight. Listening to her movements, he waited for her to return. It took her ten minutes in total to get ready. She skipped downstairs still with a smile on her face.

If it wasn't for the fact he couldn't smell them on her, he'd be sure she was taking drugs with her sudden happiness.

"Why are you so cheery all of a sudden?" he asked, opening the front door.

"I don't know. I'm just feeling happy for a change." She shrugged, heading out. He couldn't help but watch her ass when she stepped in front of him. Taking a jacket for her to wear, he took her hand. He was surprised when she didn't try to brush off his touch. Something had happened last night to Kitty. He didn't know what it was, but he was grateful for the change. She seemed more open, more willing to listen to him.

"You live in a beautiful place," she said.

"Thank you. Living in the middle of nowhere has its uses. No one stops by unexpectedly, and there are rumors lurking about vicious wolves." Roy smiled.

"Are they real rumors?"

"Not really. We've never killed any humans if that's what you're worried about." He let out a sigh, breathing in the air. "This is where we belong. Our home."

"It must be nice to have a home."

He scented the pain coming from her. "I'm sorry about your mother. Your father really couldn't help you?"

"No. My father hated responsibility. He left us the moment it got too hard for him. It was me and my mom for so long." She glanced down at the ground.

"We're your family now, Kitty. I know it seems

like a lot to take in. A couple of months ago you didn't know werewolves existed, and now you're living with them and they're intending to mate with you. It's a lot to take in."

Tightening his grip around her hand, he gave her a little smile. This was the longest he'd been away from his brothers since they were all born.

"Do you want to mate with me?" she asked, taking him by surprise once again.

"Me?"

"Yes, Tom took me, and it was almost as if it was agreed that you all wanted me. None of us got a choice in this. Do you really want me?"

Stopping, Roy turned to stare into her eyes. They were clear, blue, and filled him with utter rapture. "You don't think I want you?"

****

Tucking some hair behind her ear, Kitty chanced a look at the ground. Looking anywhere but at Roy felt like the safest option to her. That morning she woke up determined to start anew. She hated feeling like a spare part, being used to help a bunch of brothers. Family meant everything to her, and seeing as she didn't have any of her own anymore, as her father didn't count, she'd do anything to help a family keep together.

The Snows may be wolves, but they were brothers. In the few weeks she'd seen them all together she knew they shared a special bond, a sacred bond. They were prepared to share her for the sake of such a bond.

"Tom took me from a bus stop, Roy. He took me, and you, along with your other brothers, were not given a choice. You're picking me out of all of those women." Kitty wasn't anything special. She was blonde, full figured, and had nothing particular to offer them. Her life hadn't been full and exciting. She'd loved her mother, and that was all. "There is a world full of women. How do I know you're not going to regret this in a few years' time? You're settling with me."

He sank his fingers into her hair and started walking her back.

"Roy?" He didn't answer, and she only stopped moving when a tree stopped her. The rough bark did little to soothe her thoughts, but Roy wouldn't hurt her. She was sure of that.

"Do you think as wolves, paranormal beings, we can settle for anyone?" he asked.

She frowned. "I was the first available woman."

"Baby, mating is more than just being available." He leaned in close, and she heard him give her a sniff. All of the men took to sniffing her before Roy took the first moon.

"Why do you keep sniffing me?"

"Destined mates carry a certain smell. I've been with hundreds of women, Kitty. I've had them all begging for my cock and screaming for me to take them. I've taken human women and wolf women. None of them hold your scent."

"My scent?" She was starting to sound like a broken record. None of his words were making any sense to her.

He cupped her face, his thumb running along her lip.

"I can't stop looking at you, Kitty. Your hair is like gold to me. When I look into your eyes, I see the ocean and know I could live a lifetime of torture and misery, if I got to look into your eyes every day."

She gasped at the picture he painted. His breath fanned her face.

"You're absolutely beautiful. I see the kindness in

your eyes and the happiness on your face. I know I want to be one of the reasons to put that smile on your face." His lips nibbled along her collarbone.

Heat flooded her panties at his words. They were amazing, romantic even.

"Then we get to your body. Your tits fill my hand, and you've got the tightest, reddest nipples I've seen." To emphasize his words, he cupped her breasts, thumbing the tips.

Crying out, she arched her back, needing more of his touch.

"Down we go to your waist and your hips make me want to fuck you so hard. I imagine holding onto your hips, bruising them as I pound away inside you but keep you still to take my cock."

She whimpered. Kitty wanted that. She wanted to be at his mercy as he took his pleasure.

"Your ass is ripe for the taking. Your pussy is always wet. I can smell your need right now, baby. You want a good hard fucking, don't you?" he asked.

"Yes," she said, whispering the word. She was melting, craving his touch more than anything else.

"This is not all, Kitty. Your scent, it calls to me." He closed his eyes, and she watched him inhale. "I feel the wolf inside me. He wants to mate with you, fuck you, claim you." When he opened his eyes, they were a darker shade of hazel and his pupils were larger than ever before. "I want to share you with my brothers and claim you as mine along with the rest of them. They were my family as you will be."

He tilted her head back so he looked deep into her eyes.

"What do you want, Roy?" she asked.

Her body was alive for him. Everything else faded away as he stared into her eyes.

"I want to give you everything your heart desires. I never want to see you hurt or go without. When the time comes, it's going to tear me apart." He silenced her with a finger against her lips. "No, we're not going to speak of what's going to happen. Two weeks. We've got two weeks until the pull of the moon will bring us together and pull us apart."

Roy took her lips, silencing her further.

She moaned, and he took advantage to plunder her mouth with his tongue.

"Give me your kisses, baby. I can give you so much pleasure. You don't even know what you're missing out on. I promise."

Kitty gave herself over to the pleasure of his mouth. His hands moved up and down her body. She couldn't contain her pleasured cries for much longer. Whimpering, she circled his neck, holding onto him.

"No," he said, minutes later.

She was burning up, ready to give him everything he ever wanted. Instead, he broke away from the kiss and took a step back.

"We're going to do this properly." He wrapped his arms around her, dropping a kiss to her nose. "You're going to know what it means to be loved by one of the Snow men. No sex, no expectations, just romance."

Whatever he was going to do, Kitty was excited. She'd never been dated by a guy, and she'd never fallen for one, apart from Tom, but she looked forward to Roy showing her what it was all about.

Chapter Four

The next two weeks were a complete dream. Roy spent every available moment convincing Kitty of his feelings and showing her what it meant to be truly wanted and desired. He tortured himself by staying away. She didn't deserve to be rushed into anything. Roy didn't need time to think about his feelings. Her scent, her personality, everything about her pulled him in.

When he was around her, he was like a moth to a flame. Her entire aura burned brighter than any sunlight that he knew. Sitting across from her, he watched her tongue peek out the side of her mouth as she decided where to move. They were playing a game of chess and he could defeat her in three short moves, but he loved to watch her think it out. She took everything so seriously. Their time was running out, and before long he'd take her out into the night with the moon riding high in the sky. He would make love to her, claiming her for himself and for his wolf.

Cutting off the thoughts, Roy couldn't bring himself to think about walking away. Once he claimed her and she accepted his claiming, he had to walk off and leave for the next man to make his claim.

In the forest, his brothers would be there, watching, waiting. When it was all over and she watched him leave, one of them would come up and embrace her. Then the cycle started again.

Last chance.

Shaking his head, he glanced up to see Kitty watching him. She must know their time was fast coming to an end. In the last two weeks he'd spent every available moment telling her how much he loved her while she hadn't spoken the words to him.

Part of him was terrified. If one of them was to

fail then the claiming stopped altogether. The curse of the wolf would be complete, and they'd be bound to their wolves, never allowed to roam the world as a man.

"Are you okay? You've gone really quiet. It's kind of scary after you've done nothing but talk," she said, moving her knight.

He saw she was about to go into checkmate but decided not to end the game too soon.

"I talk because you like being quiet."

"No, you've got a lot more fun tales to tell about your brothers. I'm going to tell them all, you know, how you used their misfortune to seduce me."

Roy chuckled as she waggled her brows, conspiring against him.

"Kitty, you know—"

She cut him off by holding up her hand. "I know what is going to happen tomorrow night, Roy. I can read a calendar and know our time together is coming to an end." She stared down at her hands. "I don't have to like what's going to come. I'm going to miss you."

His heart soared.

"You've liked our time together?" he asked.

"I've never laughed so much in my life. When you actually put the effort in, you were amazing to be with, Roy."

Tears glistened in her eyes, and he felt like a total bastard. All he could think about was his own needs and feelings.

"Don't cry, baby."

Getting up from his seat on the floor, he rounded the table and wrapped his arms around her. She settled back against him, and his cock hardened at the feel of her. Apart from the odd kiss, neither of them had touched intimately. They cuddled together watching movies but nothing else. This was their first time really touching since he'd last taken her, and he was ready to fuck her again.

His cock was begging, and his wolf was so close to the surface, he threatened to split his skin ready to get out to her.

"It's going to happen again, isn't it?" She ran a hand over her face as she turned her head against his chest. He held her tight as she sighed. "No, I can't do this." She pulled out of his arms, and he watched her put away their unfinished game of chess. He hated this. Causing her pain was never his intention.

Following her through to the kitchen, he watched her lean against the sink with her back to him.

"It's the full moon tomorrow."

"I know. You need me to let the claiming happen." She turned toward him. "I get what I need to do. Tom let me know, and I thought I understood everything that is going on, but I don't, do I? There is a lot more going on here than any of you are telling me."

Roy gritted his teeth. "I cannot tell you what you want to know. I love you, Kitty, and I wish I could spare you this pain, but I can't." He reached out, touching her shoulder. For two weeks he'd not touched her, and now he didn't want to stop.

After tomorrow night he wouldn't get to see her until the next claiming, and he certainly wouldn't get to be with her until Tom completed the claiming and they all possessed her. Only when they all claimed her would he get the chance to be with her forever.

"You can't do any of these things."

She turned back to him, wiping her hands on a towel. Tears were in her eyes, but they hadn't fallen down her cheeks. He watched her fight to keep her emotions at bay.

Caressing her face with his knuckles, he felt his

heart ache for her.

"No, I can't help you. What I can do is tell you how I feel and what I want to do with you. Our time together is not over. We've got a lifetime together."

"How many women have failed to complete the claiming?"

"None. It's an emotional process, baby. We don't know what you're going through, but we're going through something similar. I promise you, we're not going away unscathed by this process."

She looked somewhere past his shoulder. He wished he knew what was going on through her mind. "I'm sorry. It's silly, these thoughts and feelings."

"No, it's not silly. These thoughts are part of you. I never want you to feel something and be afraid to tell me." Leaning down, he pressed his lips to hers. "When all of this is over you can come to me and I'll protect you."

****

Roy's kiss made Kitty tingle all over. In two weeks he'd invaded her heart, and now she was scared about what was to come. Watching him walk away was going to hurt something deep inside her. She didn't know how other women survived this kind of torture. Falling in love, making love, and watching the man that had come to mean so much to you leave was so hard.

"Go to bed, baby. It's late, and you need your sleep."

Nodding, she pressed another kiss to his lips and made her way upstairs.

She stared for the longest time at her reflection in the mirror. Her skin looked pale and her eyes wide.

Touching her lips, she closed her eyes imagining Roy in the bathroom with her. When she could no longer feel his touch, she opened her eyes, removed her clothing and stood under the warm water of the shower.

Give yourself to him.

You're in love with him and the Snow men already.

They've given you so much in such a short time.

Kitty pushed the thoughts away as she remembered the feeling of Tom walking away after he'd taken his pleasure.

He gave you pleasure as well.

Her thoughts were always her downfall.

Once she was finished in the shower, she turned off the heat and went back into the bedroom. Using one of Roy's old shirts, she placed it over her head and sat on the edge of the bed.

Tomorrow night, after the claiming finished, she would be with a new man.

This is Roy's last night.

Running a hand down her face, she got to her feet before she cowardly went to bed. She made her way downstairs. Roy's grunts met her ears, and she took her time to get to him. From the position near the sitting room door, she saw he was naked and he had his large erection in his hand. In the low light she saw the top glistened with his pre-cum. His eyes were closed, and she gasped at the desperation on his face.

The sound of her gasp forced him to open his eyes. The moment he saw her, he stopped touching himself.

She shook her head. "No, don't stop. Touch yourself. I want to watch."

Entering the room, she took a seat opposite him so she got a perfect view of him playing.

"Fuck, Kitty, I'm sorry."

"Don't be sorry. Please, let me see you do this."

Resting her hands on her knees, she felt an

answering heat spill between the lips of her pussy. Licking her suddenly dry lips, she watched his hand, which was shaking, grip his shaft.

He let out a groan. His fingers smeared the pre-cum around the tip then down the sides. Roy groaned, and the noise sent another wave of heat through her.

Her nipples tightened against the fabric of the shirt.

"What made you touch yourself?" she asked, intrigued.

"You. Your kiss. The scent of you fills the cabin, and you make me ache."

Standing up, she removed the shirt she wore. Naked, she gave him a turn feeling sexy as he gazed at her hungrily. "Does this help?"

"More than you fucking know." He gripped the base of his cock and moved up to the tip then back down again. She watched him fuck his fist while his gaze ate her up. Feeling empowered she sat down on the edge of the sofa, splaying her thighs wide for him to see her sex. "Fuck me."

Smiling, she watched his movements. The way he gripped the length of his shaft and the cum spilling from the tip. Everything about him was intoxicating.

"Touch yourself, Kitty. Let me see you spill that sweet juice over your fingers."

Caressing her fingers up the inside of her thigh, she cupped her mound and slid a finger through her slit. She was soaking wet to the touch. No wonder she was so wet. Roy, masturbating, was a beautiful sight. He made her want, and she wasn't leaving until she saw him spill his cum all over his stomach.

He leaned back as she glided a finger over her clit.

"When all of this is over I'm going to spend

weeks loving your pussy and showing you how much I fucking hated this. I love you, Kitty. No other woman would ever satisfy this need I've got for you. I can't wait to have you as my mate."

She whimpered and pressed two fingers inside her body, caressing her clit with her thumb.

"Fuck, I'm not going to last. Watching you is a fucking dream."

Keeping her eyes on him, she saw his movements speed up. A musky scent filled the room, and she moaned at the smell.

"Fuck, baby, come. Let me see you lose yourself in pleasure."

Kitty watched him as her orgasm crashed through her, sending her over the edge into a beautiful kind of bliss. All through it, she watched him stroke his cock.

When she was done, she kept her fingers inside her watching as he growled. The tip spurted out white strands of his cum, which coated his stomach.

Collapsing against the sofa, she saw him get to his knees and start to crawl toward her.

"Give me your fingers," he said.

Pulling her fingers out of her cunt, she presented them to his lips.

Roy sucked them inside, moaning as he licked her cream from each digit. "You taste fucking amazing."

He used his shirt to wipe the semen from his stomach. Smiling, she leaned her head back.

"It's time for bed, baby."

She took hold of his hand and tugged him to his feet. "Come with me to bed. I don't want to go without you."

Staring into his eyes, she saw he was torn over what to do. Go with her or stay behind and risk hurting her.

"After what we just shared I want to feel your arms around me for one last night." Kissing his lips, she smiled. "I just want you to hold me. Can you do that, Roy?" she asked.

"I could hold you all night long."

Settling down into bed, she felt complete having Roy's arms around her. For a few short hours she could forget what would happen tomorrow night.

Chapter Five

The moon was high in the sky. Roy stared up at the glowing sun, wishing there was some way to make tonight more bearable for his woman. Kitty was his woman. When the time came, he was going to make up for what he was going to do on this very night. His brothers were close by to offer him support. Their presence grew closer with every passing second. The light in the bedroom of the cabin glowed, letting him know Kitty was getting ready for the claiming.

"There has to be another way to do this?" Roy asked minutes later as Tom appeared from behind one of the trees.

"They are the rules, Roy. Do you think it doesn't cut me up and hurt me to know she's hurting? It pains me to see her or to even feel her like this." Tom pressed a hand to his heart. "When tonight is over, you'll feel her, too. You'll know what it's like to feel her pain, and you can't do anything to stop it. This is the cruelty, the harshness I told you about. There is no stopping what is about to happen."

Growling, Roy turned away to see Guy stepping closer. "You're taking her next?"

"Yes. I'm taking her next. Then Stuart will take her, followed by the twins. They are bound by one moon to make this claiming right. When they're finished, Tom will bind us all to her, and the claiming will be finished," Guy said.

"When it is all done, we will live in peace, begging for Kitty's forgiveness," Roy said.

The wolf inside him was begging to get out. He wanted to run, but first he wanted to claim what was rightfully his.

"You will all be there tonight?" he asked.

"Yes, you know we have to be there for the claiming. You will fuck her, bite her, and then like me, you'll walk away leaving Kitty to Guy," Tom said.

Turning around he looked at Guy, who was looking at the ground.

"You better treat her with the utmost care and attention. I will not have her scared or in pain." Roy was shaking as a sickness swamped him.

"She's my mate, too. Do you think I don't feel responsible for her pain? It took you over two weeks to get close to her. How long do you think it will take me?" Guy asked.

"Look, this is difficult for all of us," Stuart said, stepping up close. Joey and Mark followed suit.

"Difficult. How can you even get your head out of a book long enough to know what is difficult and what is not?" Roy shouted the words, storming toward his brother.

"Enough!" Tom, the wolf, bellowed the words out, and Roy had no choice but to stop. "This claiming is vital to all of us. Our wolves are growing closer. To stay this way all of us have to play our part. None of us like this, but it's who we are."

Glancing around at his brothers, Roy watched as all of them stepped back, listening to their alpha. They would all soon share a mate. This was not the time or place to argue about what they wanted to do.

"I'm sorry," Roy said, looking at each of them in turn. "None of us knew how this would feel." He turned to Guy. "She's going to be distraught. Don't give her chance to hate us. Embrace her, love her, and you'll see what a treasure she is."

The sound of the cabin door opening filled his senses. An explosion of smell met his nose. She was near, and she was ready to become his mate. Pride filled him at her coming out. He expected to wait half the night before she came to him.

"I'll see you soon," Roy said, looking at Tom.

They all nodded, and he left them alone in the forest.

Making his way to where Kitty waited, Roy emerged to see her standing, waiting for him, naked. Her full figure was a sight to behold. Full tits, flared hips, and a nice rounded stomach were what he craved to keep him comforted at night.

"Hey," she said, tucking some of her hair behind her ear.

Roy didn't stop walking until he had Kitty in his arms. Sinking his head against her skin, he inhaled her scent. Home, she smelled like home to him.

"I love you, Kitty."

She didn't say anything to him. Her arms held him tighter, and he was sure he detected a sob coming from her lips.

Pulling away, he stared down into her eyes.

"What's the matter, baby?" he asked.

"Make love to me, Roy. Take me as your mate."

Caressing her cheek, he claimed her lips once again, taking his time. She worked on his jeans, pushing them down his thighs until he stood before her naked.

Sinking his fingers into her hair, he growled when she circled his shaft with her fingers. Her touch alone threatened to set him on fire. He was already close to orgasm just from the sight of her alone.

Running his hands up and down her body, he gripped her hair to tilt her head back, exposing her neck.

His cock hardened even more, the tip leaking out his fluid into her waiting hand. Breaking away from her touch, he took her hand and pulled her down onto the earth beside him. The smell of the grass along with her arousal was a heady thing.

Roy took his time, caressing every inch of her flesh, drawing her to new, dizzying heights.

"Roy?"

"Don't worry about a thing, baby. I'm going to take care of you."

Sliding his fingers through her slit, he felt her heat coating his hand. He stroked her clit watching the pleasure fill her eyes. She opened her legs wide for him to play with her body.

"That's it, baby. Give me everything.

Roy felt the need to claim her rise up. His brothers were close, and the claiming need inside them rose. He felt all of them and their need to claim Kitty.

Teasing her clit, he waited until he hurtled her into a mind-shattering orgasm before he settled between her thighs.

****

Roy's brothers were not hidden from Kitty's view. The bite on her neck heated, and she became aware of all brothers around her, even Tom. He was in the forest watching as Roy took her body. The orgasm shattered her mind, opening up her senses for her to feel all of the brothers.

Staring at Roy she felt him move between her thighs. The tip of his cock rubbing through her slit, coating his shaft with her cream.

"I love you, Kitty."

She believed him. In their month he'd proven to her more than once that he was in love with her. Smiling, she reached up to touch his cheek.

"I love you, too." Kitty spoke the words she'd kept away from him for so long.

He plundered her pussy going to the hilt inside her.

"Fuck, you're so tight."

Wrapping her arms around his body, she held on tightly as he started to pound away inside her. Roy didn't stop in his possession. He pulled out only to slam in deep. She was so wet that he glided through her easily.

He took hold of her hands and pressed them to the earth beside her head.

"Kitty Evans, you are mine as I am yours. Nothing will tear us apart. I mate with you. Please accept my life and my protection as yours."

His words had her gasping as his cock swelled within her.

"Yes, I accept your claiming and your love." She sank her nails into his hands. He leaned down, sinking his canines into the flesh of her neck.

Crying out, she felt her blood flowing into his mouth, and then he pulled away, biting into his palm before pressing his wrist to her mouth. She sucked down his blood, feeling the claiming take over.

Her body heated, and everything came alive at his taste. The scent of the earth, the grass, and of his brothers overflowed all of her senses.

Staring left and right she watched his brothers come closer. They were no longer hiding. They all surrounded them as Roy offered up her blood for them to taste. Each of them licked her life's essences, filling themselves with her.

Heat spilled between her thighs as Tom was the last. She moaned, and Roy pumped in deep inside her. He covered her body, his lips against her ear.

"I promise you, I love you. I'll never leave you, and you'll be in my heart for the rest of our life."

She nodded, knowing their moment was fast coming to an end. The heat flowed through them all. In that one moment she felt all of the brothers and their wolves, embracing her.

Guy stayed close to them. His dark hair was cut short, and his eyes glowed amber as he looked at her. He stroked her hair as Roy pumped inside her, going deeper than ever before.

"I love you, Kitty."

"I love you, Roy. I give myself to you." She gave in, opening up her mind as Roy tensed. His cock jerked inside her, and the heat of his semen filled her body. Crying out, she stared up at the full moon. The warmth glowed over her skin.

Their connection was not lost, but she knew it was going to happen any second.

His orgasm stopped, and his cock went flaccid.

Still, he did not leave her body.

"Roy, you know what you've got to do," Tom said.

Tensing, Kitty withdrew as Roy pulled away from her. His gaze didn't stay on her as he left her body. The moment he was gone, she felt empty inside. This was what she hated and didn't know if she could stand to live through again.

When Roy did finally look at her, she saw the pain in his gaze. He didn't want to do this either.

He took another step back, and she watched his human form fall away, giving way to the beautiful hazel colored wolf.

"Roy?" She spoke his name, hoping he'd come to her.

Even in wolf form, he took a step back, refusing her.

Tears spilled down her cheeks, and Guy's arms surrounded her. "I've got you, pet. He needs to do this."

She didn't look away from where Roy had claimed her. His brothers were still there. Getting to her feet, she looked at each of them. Guy reached out to her, but she pushed him away, slapping his hands when he made to touch her.

"Kitty," Tom said, moving forward.

Shaking her head, she looked at each of them in turn. Guy, Stuart, Mark and Joey, how much pain did they expect her to go through? She was a human. Being fucked and watching them walk away was not fun for her. Kitty hated it. She hated every second that they used her.

They're not using you. They're mating with you.

She didn't care. In that moment, it felt too much like being used.

Stepping away, she made her way back to the cabin.

"Kitty," Tom said. Spinning around, she shot him a glare.

"You do not get to speak to me." Pointing a finger at him, she made her way back toward the cabin. Slamming the front door, she didn't care if she pissed Guy off.

Twice she'd been fucked, and twice she had to watch the men leave her without a backwards glance.

It hurt.

Walking upstairs, she climbed into the bed and wrapped the blanket around her.

How did women survive this?

They had to have survived, as otherwise the Snow brothers wouldn't be here. Closing her eyes, she counted numbers in her head trying her hardest to stop the pain.

The claiming mark on her neck dripped her blood onto the pillow as his semen coated the tops of her thighs.

"Kitty," Guy said, trying the door. "I can break the door down if I want."

"Leave me alone."

"Pet, I know this is hard."

Grabbing the lamp at the side of the bed, she threw it at the door. "You know nothing. Leave me alone."

Collapsing to the bed, Kitty let the tears fall. How was she going to survive at least three more moons of this?

No answer came, but she did know one thing. She couldn't walk away from them.

Epilogue

Guy ran fingers through his hair as he made his way to the big house. Kitty was locked in her bedroom at the cabin and wouldn't see him. It had been two days since Roy's claiming, and she still hadn't eaten. She wouldn't see him, talk to him, or have anything to do with him.

This was a lot harder than he'd anticipated.

Roy was sat on the steps leading up to the house looking like hell.

"How is she?" Roy asked.

Tom, Stuart, and the twins came out of the house waiting.

"She won't have anything to do with me. I can't get her to eat or to see me. I hear her crying."

His brothers were instantly filled with pain. They had all heard tales of women struggling through a pack claiming, especially one with brothers.

"You've got to take care of her," Roy said.

"It's hard to take care of a woman who wants nothing to do with me." Resting hands on his hips, Guy looked at his brothers hoping they had ideas.

"We're counting on you," Tom said.

"I know." Guy stared at all of them. "Have you ever tried seducing a woman who is bleating for your brother?"

"Yes," Roy said, shouting. "I did it when she was mourning Tom. For fuck's sake, don't fuck this up."

"What do you expect me to do?"

"Take her out climbing. Go in and take her," Stuart said. "We've got no choice. We can't restart this shit again. She's our last hope."

Blowing out a breath, Guy moved past his

brothers going into the house. "Fine, I'll do what I can, but none of you interfere with my methods. I'm going to woo her the way *I* would."

Thirty minutes later, Guy was packed and ready to take Kitty away from the pain she'd come to associate with the cabin and the house.

His brothers asked him questions, which he ignored.

Going to the cabin, he walked inside smelling Kitty's pain. He loved her, and yet they'd rarely spoken. This was the curse of becoming mated as a pack. They all fell for the woman at the same time. From the moment Tom brought her home, he'd been in love with her.

He walked up the stairs, knocked on the door waiting.

"Go away."

The pain in her voice was too much.

He kicked the door down. He'd leave the mess for one of his brothers to clean up.

She squealed, jumping up from the bed.

"I know you're hurting, but I'm not going to let you waste my fucking month."

Guy grabbed a pair of jeans and a shirt from the nearest drawer.

"You're insane and completely crazy."

Throwing the clothes at her, he stared into her eyes. They were red rimmed and swollen from all the crying. "Get dressed. We're going out, and I won't hear any complaints from you." He turned away heading out of the room to give her privacy. Glancing back, he smiled. "You will leave this bedroom, Kitty. If I have to come and get you, I'll spank your hot little ass to get what I want."

He left to the sound of her muttering curses at

him.

The End

SAM CRESCENT

SECOND SIN

The Pack Claims a Mate, 3

Sam Crescent

Copyright © 2015

Chapter One

"Are you for real? This is supposed to be your idea of wooing me?" Kitty asked, stepping over another branch. They were walking through the forest. She had a giant bag on her shoulders while Guy was several steps ahead of her.

"What's the matter, Kitty? Doesn't this fit in with your plans of mourning one brother?" He didn't look back but kept on walking.

They'd been walking for the past three days, and she wasn't any closer to feeling happy about it. Her feet hurt, and so did her heart. Being claimed by six brothers wasn't as fun as many would believe. After being used by Tom, and watching him walk away, then Roy do the same, her heart was just hurting every step of the way. She stopped and glared at Guy.

"Is this just a game to you?" she asked, gripping the handles of her bag. "Tire out the human so she stops her moaning?"

Guy stopped, turning around to look at her. He moved quickly pressing her up against a tree. "You don't think we're suffering?" he asked, grabbing her hands and shoving them above her head.

Kitty didn't understand why he was restraining her when she wasn't actually fighting him. She shook her head, licking her dry lips. "How can you be suffering?"

"I can't speak for all my fucking brothers, but let's get one thing straight. We're destined to mate to one woman. That woman being you. The next couple of months you've got to fall for each of us, spending time and falling in love. You don't know me, and you're in love with not one but two of my brothers. While I've got you in my arms, with the scent of your pain between us, I know you're in love with both of them. In order for this claiming to work, you've got to fall for all of us." He pushed his face against her neck, and she listened as he took a deep inhalation. "You smell so good. I can't wait for us to claim you completely. The moment we do, there's not going to be any holding back. You'll be our mate, and know it kills us to walk away from you."

"Guy?"

"You're not the only one suffering here. My brothers are suffering. Tom and Roy, they're in pain because you're hurting. Stuart, Mark, and Joey, they're all scared because if they don't mate properly with you, we all suffer."

His hands squeezed a little tighter around her wrists before he finally pulled away. "We want to make this work. You're our mate, Kitty. Watching you give up part way through the month, isn't something that's easy for us."

She'd not thought about their pain, only her own. "I'm sorry."

"I'm doing something different from both of my brothers, and I'm doing it so that you're not reminded of them. I know the forest will remind you of them because

we're all wolves, but it doesn't have to be a problem."
He cupped her cheek, running his thumb across her
cheek. "You're so beautiful."

In that moment, she felt beautiful to him. "I'll try
to make this better. I'm really sorry."

"Don't be. We're all trying to adapt to a lot of
change. That main change being the fact we're all going
to be mated for life."

"Are you sure I'm your true mate? Surely you
could find any woman."

Guy stared at the ground. "Do you want to keep
moving?"

"If we're not staying here overnight then yes. The
ground is, erm, really alive."

She saw it practically moving with creepy
crawlies. There was only so much insect life she could
stand.

"Come on." Guy took her hand, and they started
moving back through the forest. She liked his grip, the
firmness of his hand within hers. Licking her lips, she
took a deep breath changing a glance toward him. Guy
was different from Roy and Tom. He wasn't as large as
the other two men, but there was something earthy about
him. The way he moved through the forest, she knew he
was at home here, rather than in the comfort of the house.
"You're our true mate. We have tried to mate other
females, but they were females we had brought home,
not one that Tom had picked. He's our alpha, our oldest
brother, and so, he has the higher senses in everything."

"Doesn't that bother you?"

"When I was younger I thought it was a raw deal.
Tom got to pick everything, and I just had to fall in line.
The truth is, Tom has all of the responsibility. It's down
to him that we survive, that we thrive as a pack, and that
when another pack comes, we can fight to protect what is

ours."

"Have you ever been in battle?" she asked.

"No. We train for battle, but most of the packs know not to invade another pack's land." He squeezed her hand. "We all work the land, and Stuart, the bookworm, he works the stock markets. We earn enough money that we pay our taxes and we don't need to venture out."

Kitty nodded. "I don't need money to help me make a decision."

"What made you not run from us? A lot of women would be terrified to be around one wolf, let alone a pack of brothers."

She didn't answer straight away as they had to climb over a fallen tree. It was too thick, and it required Guy to jump over first then help her with his hands on her waist. Her shirt slid up, and the warmth of him touched her bare skin. She gasped at the contact, shocked by the power his touch had over her.

"What is it?" he asked. "Did something stick inside you?" He turned her and began patting and caressing her body. She'd never been more mortified in her life. He took a deep sniff and glanced up at her. "You're aroused."

"You don't need to be so blunt about it." Her cheeks were on fire with embarrassment. What was wrong with these men?

"I like it. You smell so damn hot." He groaned, running his nose against her neck, and using his mouth to kiss the whole of her body.

She bit her lip trying to contain her need by crossing her legs.

"Don't," he said, pushing his palm between her thighs.

Kitty took a deep breath. All of her pain seemed

to evaporate at Guy's touch. She wanted more.

****

She was so damned hot between the thighs, it was taking every ounce of Guy's control not to throw her to the ground and fuck her hard. He'd been fighting the need from the moment it was his turn to claim her. The moment Roy was mated to her, he'd felt the pull to do the same, to claim her, to take her, and cherish her.

"Tell me to fucking stop," he said, growling out each word.

"Why the hell would I tell you that?" she asked, licking those fuckable lips again.

Every time she licked her goddamned lips, it tested his limits of control. Finally, he held her attention, and she was aroused because of him.

"If you're not ready for me to take you, then tell me to stop." He needed to be inside her, to know what her warm, wet, cunt would feel like wrapped around his cock.

"I don't want you to stop, Guy. Please, I want to be with you." She ran her hands up his chest, going to his neck. There was only so much he could handle before he caved in. Wrapping his hands around her waist, he pulled her in close, moaning as her curvy body pressed against his. She was so damn perfect, and she took his breath away every time he got close to her. This was what he'd been waiting for, searching for, a chance to connect to this woman on a basic, hungry level.

He didn't have to mate with her, but he could still fuck her.

If there was one thing Guy knew, it was how to fuck. Tugging his backpack off his shoulders, he turned her around doing the same so that they were both free.

Taking her down to the forest floor, he followed her down, landing between her spread thighs. She was so damn hot between her legs. Guy tugged out of her hair the band that was holding the strands bound in a ponytail. He ran his fingers through the length, loving the feel of the silky blonde tresses gliding through them. Finally, he gripped her hair tight in his fist before slamming his lips down on hers.

She moaned, sinking her own fingers into his hair, holding him close. Kitty held him close, rubbing her pussy all over his dick. It didn't matter that they were covered in clothes. The whole feel of her body wrapped around him was enough to drive him crazy. Pressing his tongue into her mouth, he tasted his mate, the pack mate, and felt at home. His cock pulsed inside his pants, needing out and inside her.

"Please, Guy, I need you. I need more." She released a little whimper, which was more than he could bear.

He pulled away, tugging his shirt off his body. Kitty sat up on the ground, and began to remove her own clothing. He stopped her with a hand on hers. "No, let me do it."

Guy took over, lifting her shirt over her head, then flicking the catch on her bra, exposing her beautiful, large tits. She was a dream come true, so lush and ripe. Some men loved women who were slender, but he was a curves man all the way. There was just something about gripping onto a nice pair of thick hips that had his dick aching and hard, ready to fuck.

"Lie back," he said. He'd moved them far enough away so she wasn't touching anything gross or muddy. Guy understood about a woman's particular taste in the bedroom. Having a spider running over her body while he fucked her wasn't exactly going to get him the response he wanted.

She lay back, and he took the time to remove her

walking boots, followed by the long walking pants he'd given her.

Her thighs were lovely, thick, and would take the pounding he was about to give her. He couldn't wait to get inside her pussy.

With quick movements, he rid them both of their clothes, going between her spread thighs, to stare at the beauty of her cunt. She was stunning. Kitty had waxed the fine hair off her lips. He didn't know if she'd done it before Tom and Roy, or after. He really didn't give a fuck. She was finally his, wet and waiting for him.

Opening the lips of her sex, he latched onto her clit, sucking her large nub into his mouth. Kitty screamed, sinking her fingers back into his hair. He relished the tug and refused to stop until he had her climaxing on his tongue.

Back and forth, he caressed over her sweet nub, glancing up in order to watch her come apart. Her eyes kept opening and closing, so he got a glimpse of the shocking blue that stared down at him, filled with lust.

That's right, baby. I'm the one licking your clit. I'm the one giving you pleasure.

It was all him.

Moving his finger to her entrance, he circled her hole watching her chest rise and fall, getting more erratic as he waited to penetrate her. He wasn't ready to fuck her yet. She'd have to do with his finger inside her pretty pussy.

Only when her gaze landed on him and stayed on him did he reward her by slamming his finger deep inside her cunt.

She screamed, closing her eyes, and he paused.

Once she realized he wasn't moving, her gaze fell back on him.

Flicking her clit, he waited, tormenting her, and

seeing if she'd understood that he was the one who held the power in this moment. He alone could make her come but only if she was a good girl first.

Chapter Two

Kitty groaned in frustration as the pleasure began to build only to stop whenever she looked away or closed her eyes. He was doing it on purpose, and it wasn't fair, not to her at least.

"You know what I want."

She stared down at him, and he sucked her clit back into his mouth, flicking over the bud with his tongue. It was so amazing she didn't want it to end. Closing her eyes, she tilted her head back, and ... he stopped. She'd never known torture like it.

Opening her eyes, she stared down at him. He did the same, teasing her with his tongue, creating new heights of sensation. She closed her eyes only for him to stop.

He wants your eyes on him.

Staring back down at him, Guy started to tease her clit once again. She kept her gaze on him, using every ounce of strength and control that she could muster so she didn't look away from him. Biting her lip, she tried to stay focused on only him. It was so hard.

His fingers moved inside her, pumping in and out at first, and getting faster. He added a second finger inside her, making it hard for her to focus on keeping her gaze on him.

The moment she closed her eyes, he stopped. She forced them open again, watching him. There was a wicked smile on his face, and she couldn't help but smile right back at him.

He knew what he was doing, and he loved torturing her.

Kitty was desperate to come. She needed his cock inside her and his body wrapped around her.

Instead of looking away, she watched his tongue

attack her pussy, sliding up and down her slit. His fingers began to pump within her, teasing her, bringing her to life once again.

He curved his fingers around, stroking over that magical G-spot. She screamed out. The sound echoed throughout the forest. She didn't care who heard her. What Guy was doing to her pussy was so damn amazing that she refused to think of who could hear.

Tom and Roy, they'd fucked her, mated her, and left her. Now was her time with Guy. She couldn't allow the next months of her claiming to affect her so much. They were doing this to bind her to them for life. She needed to remember that each time they walked away, breaking her heart.

They were all breaking apart just as much as she was. She did see why the claiming was so important for the pack. It would bind them together forever, bringing them all love, joy, happiness, and everything in between.

"Yes, Guy," she said, moaning as he tongued her clit, and she rode his face, loving each new heightened bit of pleasure. She rubbed her pussy onto his face, sinking her fingers back into his hair. Kitty didn't have to lie down and wait for the pleasure. She was going to take what he offered, and give him back equally as much in return.

"You like me licking your pussy?"

"Yes, please, I need it. I need you to let me come." She didn't look away. Kitty had learned her lesson, and she wasn't going to stop him from licking her pussy.

"Then be a good little girl. Open your thighs. I want to get to this sweet pussy with ease." He extended his tongue, and she groaned as he moved back and forth. One of his hands had his fingers inside her while the other, opened the lips of her pussy. She saw everything he was doing, and she loved it, not wanting it to stop. "The moment you come on my tongue, I'm going to fuck you so damn hard, you're going to struggle to walk."

"Yes," she said, moaning.

It's what she wanted as well, to be fucked so damn good.

"Give yourself to me, give yourself to the pack, Kitty, and we'll treat you like a queen."

She was going to. Kitty would mate with his three other brothers, binding herself to him, and loving him for the rest of her life. She would love all six brothers, Tom, Roy, Guy, Stuart, Mark, and Joey. They would all hold a special place in her heart.

He thrust inside her, fucking her harder than ever before with his fingers. His tongue also kept flicking her clit, and it was just too much. She couldn't handle the intense pleasure coming from his hand and tongue.

"Yes, yes, yes," she said each word, panting it out.

Her orgasm spiraled closer until finally she hurtled over the edge, screaming out her climax. Kitty's entire body shook from the pressure of her release. It hadn't been that long since she last had an orgasm, but Guy did something magical with his fingers, making her forget everything else, and focus only on him.

"That's it, baby," he said, muttering the words against her clit.

Guy brought her down from her orgasm with a final flick to her clit. When it was all over she lay collapsed on the forest floor, the scent of the earth bringing her far more enjoyment than she ever thought possible.

There was no way on the planet she would have ever considered being naked in the forest with a man she barely knew, enjoyable. Yet here she was, loving every second of it.

She stared up at Guy as he moved over her. "Do you want me to get dressed?"

He looked in pain, and she smiled up at him. "Don't you dare get dressed. I want this, Guy. Don't ever be worried about wanting me. I want you. I want you so much it scares me." She leaned up, pressing her lips to his.

It was so right, that she pulled him down over her. His hands went out to rest on either side of her head. She slammed her lips up to his, smiling at the shock in his eyes.

"What's the matter?" she asked. "Never had a woman take what she wants?"

****

Guy had never wanted a woman to just take from him. He'd always been the kind of man to take control, taking what he wanted.

Kitty grabbed his arms pushing him to the ground. She gave him a smile, kissing his mouth, and biting onto his bottom lip. He growled at the bite of pain. His cock pulsed, and more of his pre-cum erupted out of the tip. She was a fucking beautiful woman. Lying down on the ground, he watched as she straddled his waist, reaching behind her to touch his cock. She rubbed the tip, smearing pre-cum onto her fingers then going to coat his shaft, making it easier for her to touch him.

"You're so hard," she said. "All of you are so damn hard, and thick."

He loved it that she referred to the pack. What he loved the most was the fact it was *his* waist she was straddling.

Running his hands up her chest, he cupped her large tits, thumbing the nipples. She arched up into his hands. He pinched her nipples, and she started to gyrate her pussy on his stomach while she worked his cock. She was soaking wet, and when he was about to take over, shoving her to the ground, and mounting her, Kitty moved down his stomach to straddle his cock.

Guy couldn't look away as she grabbed his cock, aligned the tip to her entrance, and simply slid down. She was so wet and perfect that he slid inside her with ease. He gripped her hips, loving how she filled his hands.

There were still a couple of inches to go, but he allowed her to set the pace. She took as much of him as she could handle, holding herself off him with her hands on his chest.

He caressed her body, loving every inch of her. Her tight pussy squeezed him, making it hard for him to think of anything but blowing inside her.

"You're so big," she said.

"It's all for you. Take as much of me as you can. I'm not in a rush for this to be over."

Slowly, she slid down the last few inches of his length. She took her time, rocking backward and forward. The moment he hit the hilt inside her she screamed but didn't try to pull herself off him.

"Fuck, baby. You're so tight."

"None of you are small men. I don't know if I can mate and take all six of you."

Guy smiled. All of his brothers and himself, would be taking her regularly and daily. There would be no limit to his and his brother's desires. She would constantly be having to fend them off.

"You'll learn to. We won't force you, baby." They would just be very persuasive in getting her to want to have sex with them.

"Why do I get a feeling that won't hold you back?"

"I said we wouldn't force you. I didn't say we

wouldn't try to get you to want it, too." He raised his brow at her, smiling. "We can be pretty damn persuasive."

Thrusting his hips up, he reminded her exactly how good he could be. Six of them against one, they were going to win every chance they got.

"You're not going to play fair with me, are you?"

"No. Why should we?"

Kitty took his breath away as she pulled herself up onto the tip of his cock before slamming all the way back down. He groaned, loving every second of her cunt squeezing him.

"Fuck, baby, that's it. Ride my cock. Take it deep inside your pussy."

With his grip on her hips, he fucked up to her. Guy loved the sight of her tits bouncing with each downward thrust. The sight alone was enough to make him come. It had been so long since he'd found pleasure within a woman that he couldn't hold back.

Crying out, he exploded, filling her tight pussy with his cum. Throughout his orgasm, she kept riding until he stilled her by tightening his hold on her hips.

When it was over, she collapsed over him with his cock still inside her.

Running his hands down her back, he couldn't stop touching her.

"Fuck me, that was amazing."

She chuckled. "I really am sorry."

"What about?"

"About being a bitch to you. I didn't mean it. It's just hard, and I didn't think you were going through anything like that." Kitty rested on her hands that lay on his chest.

"You're not a bitch."

"I was."

"Well, I'm not going to say anything. I've just had the best orgasm of my life." He cupped her ass groaning when her pussy clenched around his cock. "Make that the best fuck of my life."

She chuckled. "Do I have to compete with a lot of women?"

"None of them compare to you." He pushed some of her blonde hair off her shoulder. "I'm so pleased Tom found you when he did."

"Even though it's going to hurt watching you leave, I'm really glad he brought me home. You guys have saved me, and you don't even know how."

"You're an only child?"

"Yes, only child, only everything. The backpack I had when Tom brought me to the house was all I had left in the world."

"That's a nice way to say kidnapped."

Tom, the alpha and oldest brother, had kidnapped her from the bus stop, taking her home. He'd been so sure she was their mate, and he'd been right.

The truth was, they were desperate to mate. If they didn't mate now, they were going to be cursed to forever walk the earth in their wolf form. Guy loved his human body, and he had fallen in love with this human woman, their mate. "I think we can stay and make camp here."

"Are you sure?" she asked, glancing around them.

"I've got one tent. We're going to be sleeping together. Don't worry. I'll keep you warm tonight."

Chapter Three

Kitty took a bite of the sausage that Guy had held over the fire he'd built. He was an outdoorsy kind of person. She hated being outdoors most of the time. It reminded her what dangers lurked outside waiting to kill.

He's a werewolf.

"Why are you afraid?" he asked.

"It's nothing."

"Don't worry on your own. Share with me. I can be a good listener."

Taking a bite out of her sausage, she stared at him. "I was just thinking how dangerous the outside could be. It's filled with a lot of terrifying things. Then I remembered you were a wolf. The night and being outside scares me."

He wrapped his arm around her. "You don't have to be afraid with me." Guy glanced behind him, and she looked in the general direction.

"What is it?" she asked, thinking the worst. Could wolves be killed by axe wielding murderers? The very thought sent a shiver down her spine.

"Nothing, honestly. You need to stop worrying. I won't let anything happen to you." He kissed her temple. They weren't wearing any clothes, and she sat on one of the thick blankets he'd brought. It wasn't cold. There wasn't even a slight breeze, and the fire made it more than comfortable. "I can't believe I'm sitting outside naked."

"You better believe it. When we're alone like this, I'll expect you naked."

"You'll want us to do this after the mating?"

"Better believe it, baby. This isn't going to stop. All of my brothers will expect you to spend quality time with us. We're not just going to want you to perform in the bedroom. This mating, it's for life, and for love."

She stared up at him. "I love you, too, Guy."

"I didn't say I loved you," he said. "I mean, I'm not saying that I don't love you."

Kitty had come to see that Guy was more of an actions man. He didn't exactly talk much until they were having sex. They'd spent the past couple of days walking without really talking. He'd said more to her through sex at that point.

"Fine, I love you," he said.

"It's okay to talk about your feelings. I won't consider you less of a man." She snuggled up against him, seeing his cock start to lengthen. Taking another bite of her sausage she heard him moan. "I'm sure you don't want me to bite you."

"It's not your teeth, baby. I'm imagining those lips of yours wrapped around my dick."

She licked her fingers before pushing him back on the blanket. "Well, you won't have to imagine what it's like for much longer."

Gripping the base of his cock, she held the tip to her lips, and flicked the tip, swallowing down his pre-cum.

"Oh, fuck." He growled each word out. She stared up the length of his body to find his gaze riveted to where her lips were wrapped around his cock. Kitty took him to the back of her throat, sucking hard.

Guy arched up, and she saw his hand was fisted at his side. "So fucking good. Fuck. Harder."

She smiled around his shaft. Moving up his length, she licked and sucked on the tip, loving the way she was driving him crazy with her mouth. Guy was helping her to get past the hurt and to see what it meant to actually be mated to not just one brother but to six, an entire pack.

Bobbing her head to her own beat, she loved the way he clawed at the ground while she continued to suck and lick him.

"Baby, stop. I'm going to come. If you don't move I'm going to fill that beautiful mouth with cum."

Kitty kept up her pace. She wanted his cum and to taste him.

"So perfect. So right. Yes, mate."

He growled, and his cock jerked, filling her mouth with his seed. She swallowed every single drop, milking him until he tugged on her hair, pulling her away from his cock.

Resting her cheek against his thigh she took several deep breaths.

Guy picked her up in his arms, holding her close. "I have no regrets about you being my mate, Kitty. The pack, my pack, we're the luckiest bunch of bastards alive to finally have you in our lives."

She stared into the fire thinking of how lucky *she* was to have Guy, and his five brothers.

The hours passed, and after several hours of holding each other and talking, he carried her through to the tent. She wasn't tired even though they'd been walking for several miles. Rolling over to smile at him, she cupped his cheek, running her thumb along the rough flesh. He'd need to shave at some point.

"Tell me something about yourself," she said.

"I love the outdoors."

"No, something I don't know. Something no one else knows."

Guy stared up at the inside of the tent. For several minutes he didn't speak, and she was about to repeat her question when he turned toward her. "I've spent the last couple of years being afraid. Tom wouldn't venture outside for days, weeks, months on end. I didn't know if he could even leave the house at times. I didn't think he suffered with agoraphobia. I truly believe he was afraid of failing the pack. None of the brothers know I was scared that Tom would fail, that we wouldn't find you, and I wouldn't be here in this moment, holding you." He ran his hand across her waist, gripping her flesh. "This is what I was afraid of not happening."

"You've got me, and I'm not going anywhere."

"Even though we've got to mate you and leave you."

She took a deep breath. "I guess I can look forward to all of you making it up to me."

****

When Kitty was fast asleep, Guy eased her onto the blow up bed, crawling out of the tent. He loved being outdoors. To him being trapped inside a building with four brick walls was unnatural.

Moving away from the tent and their little campfire, Guy made his way toward the far left of the forest.

"You need to stop coming around, Tom."

"It's not just me," Tom said, coming out of the clearing. Roy followed behind him.

"Where are Stuart, Mark, and Joey?" Guy asked, rubbing the back of his head.

"They're back at the house. All three of them are feeling the call. It's getting closer." Tom glanced behind him.

"She's sleeping. We're almost half way through the claiming."

"We are halfway through," Tom said.

"No, I'm the halfway point. There's six of us." Guy looked toward Roy. Did they suddenly have a brother he didn't know about?

"You better tell him, Tom." Roy leaned against a

tree, looking calm and relaxed. The scent in the air was anything but calm.

"Mark and Joey are twins. Their wolves answer to each other, and so I was doing my reading, and twins are supposed to mate the woman together, during the same month. I wasn't aware of this before, but I'm aware of it now."

"The twins at the same time?" Guy asked.

"It's what it says. They can't be separated, no matter what. The bond only works with the two of them."

"Great, we mated her, and now she's got to take on the twins, as otherwise it's all for nothing."

"It's not all for nothing, Guy," Roy said. "This is for all of us."

"I can't think about this right now. I've got a couple weeks left with her, and then I've got to pass her onto boring bookworm, Stuart." Guy let out a sigh. He was really starting to struggle with the whole claiming. The love he felt for Kitty scared him. At any time she could pull away and they'd all be screwed. It wasn't just their deadline either. Guy loved Kitty. He really did love her.

"Stuart won't let us down," Tom said.

"It's easy for you to say. Have you ever seen him with a girl?" Guy asked. Out of all of the brothers, Guy couldn't even be sure if Stuart was a virgin or not. "Forget it. You need to stop lurking. This is my time with Kitty."

"We miss her," Roy said, showing the real pain he was in fact feeling.

"You don't think I know that?" he asked, getting angrier at their words. He knew all about loving someone and being afraid of losing them. Damn, he wasn't strong like his brothers. He couldn't mate with Kitty and then walk away.

You're going to have to do exactly that.

"We know you're going through hell right now. It's the same as what we're all going through," Tom said.

"What about Kitty? What about her feelings?"

"Roy and I love her already."

"What about Stuart? Will he even get his head out of a book long enough to even mate with her?" Guy was feeling protective of her. He didn't want Kitty to suffer, and part of him knew that with Stuart, she might.

She needed to be cared about, loved, taken care of—shit, all of it.

"He'll do his part. He's suffering like the rest of us, feeling the pull of the mating. Give him a chance," Tom said.

"If I discover he ignores her for a fucking book, I will beat the shit out of him and then torch every single book he owns." He stormed off, no longer wanting to be near his brothers. Guy left them behind and found Kitty in his shirt with her arms crossed over her chest. "Baby, what's the matter?"

"Why were Roy and Tom close?" she asked, shocking him.

"How did you know?"

"I felt you leave. I missed you and followed you. I couldn't hear what was being said, but it looked important."

"It's not important."

"Are you sure? It looked pretty important." She tucked some hair behind her ear, licking her lips. The sight was enough to have him groaning.

"It was nothing."

"Don't lie to me, Guy. It's not fair. I don't have your super powers, but I'm in this with you. Please, don't lie to me."

He could ignore her, or he could do what Tom

and Roy did not. "We're running out of time to complete the mating."

"What do you mean?" she asked.

"Tom came by to warn me—"

"No, you don't get to tell her," Tom said, walking through the clearing.

Guy stood in front of Kitty, protecting her. "She deserves to know the truth."

"No, this is pack business." Tom was starting to go all alpha on him, about to force his will so that he couldn't tell Kitty anything.

"Are you fucking kidding me?" Kitty asked, moving in front of him.

They were breaking a shitload of rules.

"Kitty, go inside the tent," Tom asked, authority in his voice.

"No. I'm not your brother, and I'm not part of your fucking pack. You don't get to bark orders at me as if I'm some kind of dog. I entered into this mating because I believed I was your mate. Now I find out you're holding shit back." She held her finger up, pointing at him. "You don't have the right to hold anything back. If we're going to be one big happy fucking family, then I need to start being told the damned truth."

"Kitty—"

She turned her back on Tom. "You were saying?" Guy looked over her shoulder. She snapped her fingers bringing the attention back to her. "Don't even think of looking at him for permission. You tell me the truth or I take my stuff and I walk away. I'm not bound by this mating. I can leave at any time right?"

"Will you even want to leave?" Tom asked.

She looked back at Tom.

"Do you want to test me, Tom? Right now with

all the secrets, I don't see what I'm getting out of it besides six big-headed men who need to get their heads out of their asses. Now you will tell me what the fuck is going on or I walk."

Kitty looked so damn sexy that Guy's cock pulsed to life. He wanted her badly, but he wasn't going to have her until they started telling her the truth.

Chapter Four

If Guy, Tom, and Roy didn't start talking Kitty was going to walk. She was tired of having something expected of her and being the last bloody person to know about it. Their lives were intertwined with her own. She couldn't be kept in the dark any longer.

"You're stressed," Tom said, clearly about to put her off.

Without waiting for another answer, Kitty started walking toward the edge of the forest, ready to leave. It would tear her apart to leave the three men she'd come to love so dearly. She knew it wouldn't take long for her to have the same kind of feelings about Stuart, Mark, and Joey.

"We're running out of time to complete the claiming, our mating," Roy said.

She stopped, turning around to face him. "Running out of time?"

"If we don't claim you now, with my other brothers doing their part, we will lose ourselves to our wolves, and never return to human form."

Tom growled, but she didn't care. Roy had broken rules, and he'd done it for her.

"This is your last chance to finish the claiming?" she asked. "Am I your last choice?"

"No, you're our only choice. We've only just found you. It would never have worked with any other female because *you're* our fated female. The woman destined to be ours," Tom said, finally speaking up. "We hadn't met you, and now we're running out of time."

"So, what? You came to put pressure on Guy?" she asked.

"We came to see how you're feeling," Roy said. "At least, I did. I miss you, and I worry about you."

He made to move toward her, but she held her hand up warding him off.

"No, don't come closer. This is Guy's month."

"I came to see you and to also tell Guy that Mark and Joey will have one month to mate with you," Tom said.

Whenever he opened his mouth, he was annoying her. She loved Tom, but he was so cold toward her, she really didn't know how to handle him right now.

"You've come to tell me that I've got to fuck two brothers together, to fulfill the claiming rules?" she asked. The very thought didn't offend her. She wanted to share six brothers, so two wasn't a problem to her.

"Yes."

"What rules state I've got to do all of this one on one?" She looked among the three men. "Yes, I spend the moon with one brother, but why can't I be at the house doing it? Why can't I spend time with you all but share all of my time with the one brother?" Kitty was getting frustrated with being pulled from one brother to another. It was started to grate on her nerves.

"There are no rules about it. It works better if you're alone," Tom said. "This was how we interpreted the tradition. You're not breaking any rules, providing you bond to every man within the pack."

"Then that stops now." Turning toward Guy, she closed the distance, running her hands up his chest. "I love you, and we're going to complete the mating together. We'll have many days and weeks to do this again. For the next couple of months, I need to be around all of you, to sit and eat dinner with you."

"Are you sure?" Guy asked.

"I'm more than sure. This is barbaric, taking me and leaving me. Providing I mate with each brother I don't have to be separated. If it doesn't have to be this way, then I want to change it." She ran her hands down the front of her shirt and smiled. "I guess we're trekking through the forest."

"You're not." Guy gave her his back. "Jump up. I'll carry you."

"I'm heavy."

"Don't care. Jump on and we'll walk through the forest together. Tom and Roy can carry our tent. This is still my month."

She climbed onto his back, laughing as he began walking toward the main house.

"I love this, being outdoors with you. Promise you'll always bring me with you," she said. Kitty hated the outdoors, but with Guy it made sense to her.

"I promise. You're not going anywhere without me." He held onto her legs, and she wrapped her arms around his chest, holding him close. "You really told them."

"I'm tired of being the little human stuck between six pigheaded men. I've got feelings myself. We're following a tradition that worked in the past. I want to mate with you all, and I'm not going to be a bitch about it. I can spend time with Stuart, share his bed at night, but still see you, Tom, and Roy, as well as the twins."

"Being with Mark and Joey doesn't scare you?"

"No, it doesn't scare me. What scares me is losing you to the wolf." She kissed the side of his neck, sucking on his flesh. "I can't lose you, Tom, or Roy. I'll be close with Stuart and the twins."

"Stuart is a bookworm. He concerns me."

"Why?"

This was what she loved about Guy. He was honest with her.

"He's always into his books. I don't believe he knows how to handle a woman."

"I need to be handled?"

"No, you need to be loved and cherished. That's what I do. I care about you, and I love you."

He paused at the edge of the clearing. She saw the house shining brightly.

Outside of the house, Mark and Joey were sparring with each other while Stuart read a book. The scent of a barbeque was heavy in the air.

"Wow, that smells amazing."

The moment she spoke, all three men looked toward her.

"Guy, you're breaking tradition," Stuart said, holding onto his book like it was a lifeline.

"This is all down to Kitty," he said.

"Nice, Guy, throwing me into the fire." She giggled, kissing him.

"This is Kitty's idea," Tim said.

She glanced behind her to see Roy and Tom step behind them. Now she had all the brothers in one place. No more pain, only pleasure.

****

Kitty was happy. Guy smelled it on her and felt the way her body came alive as she stared around her.

He eased her to the ground and watched Stuart, who was watching her. His younger brother stared up and down the length of her body. Stuart still held onto the book tightly, but it wasn't the same.

"I need you all to learn how to trust me, and right now, you don't. None of you really do." She looked at each of them, smiling. Guy was smitten and trusted her with his future. "This is your last chance, and I'm your mate. I can't handle being used and discarded. Providing I mate with all of you, nothing states that I can't be around you all. I'm not breaking any rules by being here." She cupped his cheek. "I'm mated to you. I'm close to you, and I know I can be close to all of you. What's to stop us from being a family? I'll share your bed until the claiming, and then I'll move into Stuart's bed. I know this has to work. I want it to work. I don't want to think of having a life without you."

"Is this allowed to happen?" Stuart asked.

Guy lifted Kitty into his arms. "It doesn't matter if it's allowed to happen or not. It's going to. And, there's nothing in the rules that states she can't do this." He moved toward the house. "Now, if you don't mind I'm going to go and spend some time with our mate."

She held onto him as he carried her into their home then upstairs toward his room. He kicked open the door, then slammed it closed with his foot. "We're all alone once again."

"What are you going to do with me?" she asked.

"First, I'm going to take you for a nice long bath." He eased her down, glancing around his space. "I'll go and run us a bath. Have a look around. See if you can see anything you like."

She smiled, and he left her alone. His heart was pounding. This was his own personal taste, light colors, and his bedroom overlooked the large forest. There was a balcony that they could sit on to watch the sunset.

Once the bath was filled with water, he walked back to his bedroom to see her looking through his movie collection.

"There are a couple of porn movies here."

"I'm a guy with needs. With you here, those will end up in the trash," he said.

She chuckled. "You're a horror movie buff?"

"Nah, I just like watching something different." He moved up behind her, wrapping his arms around her waist and pulling her in close. "You're so beautiful. Anyone ever tell you that?" he asked.

"I love you, too." She leaned back and kissed him. "I'm pleased I decided to do this, be close to all of you."

He kissed her neck. "Your bath awaits." Guy led her back toward their bathroom. He helped her out of the shirt she'd put on. She was completely naked underneath, which he loved. When he ran his hands up and down her body, she moaned.

"I love your hands on my body."

"Your body was made to be touched." He leaned, forward sucking her nipple into his mouth. Guy bit on her nipple, flicking the tip to ease out the sting.

He moved onto the next nipple, and smiled as she moaned. "Time for that bath."

She groaned but climbed into the large tub. Guy moved in behind her, holding her close.

"They were all shocked by me being here."

"You're the first woman we've known to put her foot down."

"Did you bring another woman to the pack to mate?"

"No. I did meet a woman, and I dated her for a couple of months. It didn't mean anything though. I never felt like this with her."

"Do you think Stuart, Mark, and Joey are going to like me?"

He pulled her hair out of the way, kissing her neck. "I think they're going to love you. They're not going to be able to hold back." Guy hadn't been able to hold back.

Picking up the sponge, he began to soap her body, cleaning her. In between his movements, she moaned, arching up into his touch.

"I'm sorry we cut our time together in the forest short."

"You promised me a week, baby. I'm going to hold you to it."

Guy heightened her pleasure, using every second in the bath to bring her closer to orgasm. Once the water turned cold, he carried her still dripping wet to his bed. He didn't give her a chance to turn him down. Opening her thighs, he slid between them, and finding her wet heat, he slammed inside her hard.

"Harder," she said, begging.

He took her harder than ever before. The headboard hit the wall with the force of his thrusts. Guy couldn't be without her, and he meant every word he spoke to Tom. He would beat the shit out of his three younger brothers if they ruined this for him. Kitty had stepped right out of his dreams, and was everything he wanted in a woman. Her curvy figure gave him something to hold onto, and her smile was beautiful. He didn't want to be without her in his life.

When she found her release, her pussy tightening around him, Guy followed her with his own release. Throughout it all, he held her tightly against him, never wanting to let go. The full moon was coming, and he was going to have to let her go. If she was around the house, he'd get to see her, make her smile. He didn't know how Roy and Tom put up with her being away from them. Guy knew he was never going to be as strong as his brothers.

Chapter Five

Kitty stared down at Guy's sleeping form. The last two weeks had gone by so fast, but they'd been the best two weeks of her life. Tonight was the night of the full moon where she'd mate with Guy and he'd leave her.

Grabbing a pair of jeans and one of Guy's shirts, she dressed on her way downstairs. She wanted to make him some pancakes. Like every morning, the scent of food always woke him up. Kitty entered the kitchen to find all of the brothers sat drinking and eating. They had cereal in bowls. With tonight being her last time with Guy, she wanted to make it special.

All five other brothers were nervous around her. They were worried that changing tradition would somehow affect their mating. She didn't see a problem. Kitty had spent some time looking over the pack rules, which had been kept in a diary and passed down through generations, and there was nothing in them that stated she had to be away from the whole pack during the mating. Providing she mated with each brother, there shouldn't be a problem.

"Morning," she said, moving toward the stove. She'd already explored the kitchen with Guy, and so she found a skillet, placing it on the heat.

They all said good morning to her at the same time.

She gave them each a big smile before measuring out ingredients into a bowl.

"What are you making?" Mark asked.

Out of the two twins Mark had made the effort to talk to her. Joey looked nervous as hell around her. Stuart would close whichever book he was reading to talk to her.

"I'm making some pancakes."

"You do know what tonight is, right?" Tom asked.

Glaring at Tom, she nodded. "Yes, Mr. Grumpy. I know what tonight is. You may have shocked me with the shit you pulled, but it's different now. I'm going to make this day special rather than dreading it."

"I've got the pack to think about."

"You don't think I worry about the pack? You brought me here, and now I care about you. This means the world to me. I never thought I'd ever settle down happily married. Instead, I'm going to be mated to six men who I'm coming to love. Tom, Roy, I love you, and I love Guy." She looked at Stuart. "I'm hoping to love you, and then I'm hoping to love you two guys." She turned toward the twins, smiling. "I'm sorry I can't handle being fucked and passed on. This is what I can handle. If you can't handle that, I'll leave even if it kills me."

"We don't want you to leave," Joey said. "This is hard for us all."

"Then let me make pancakes for Guy, and accept that in hours, I'm going to be mated to another man, and then I'll be with Stuart."

Looking at the bowl in front of her, she finished making the pancakes. She added some butter to a skillet before dolloping out the pancake mix.

"That smells so good," Guy said, coming into the kitchen. He wore a pair of jeans and nothing else. She smiled at him, and he didn't stop until he wrapped his arms around her waist, tugging her close. "Morning, beautiful."

"Morning."

Turning back to the skillet, she flipped the pancakes. Guy didn't leave her, instead keeping his arms wrapped around her waist, and kissing her neck.

"Do you know what tonight is?" he asked.

"I know, and I don't care. We're going to have a nice breakfast, and enjoy the rest of our day."

She made lots of pancakes, feeding all of the men, and eating a couple of pancakes drenched in maple syrup as she went, licking the stick sweetness from her fingers when she was done.

When she finished, she left the dishes to Mark and Joey, joining Guy as he walked out of the house to go and do some planting. They had a little fruit and vegetable patch a few feet from the house.

"I can't imagine going to the store every day," she said, tugging on some gloves.

"We saved a lot of money, and it gave Tom something to do with his time." Guy began to pull out the weeds that were starting to grow between the squashes, tomatoes, and herbs.

Kitty dug in helping him. She loved being in the kitchen, so this was perfect for her.

"How are you feeling?" he asked.

"I'm nervous as hell, but there's nothing we can do about it." She wasn't going to lie to him. Guy was honest with her. The least she could do was be honest with him. "What about you?"

"I want to mate with you, but I don't want to pass you off to Stuart. When it happens tonight, I want you to know it's going to tear me apart."

She smiled, trying to give him as much comfort as she could. "I understand. I understand it a hell of a lot more than you realize."

They didn't speak about what was going to happen for the rest of the day. Pushing her hair out of the way, Kitty simply enjoyed being in his company.

The day went by so quickly, and Kitty stared at her reflection in the mirror. She brushed out her hair, wearing a sexy negligee to entice Guy. Their time together wasn't enough.

When the claiming is over, you'll have him more.

Blowing out a breath, she stared at her image. Night had fallen, and the moon was high in the sky. She was already aroused at the thought of being with Guy, but she was also sad.

"Such a strange position to be in."

The sound of her door knocking invaded her thoughts. "This is it," she said.

Opening her door, she found Tom waiting for her. "Guy's waiting."

She nodded, about to pass him. Tom stopped her by grabbing her elbow. He didn't hurt her with his touch.

"I know you hate me at times, and that it's hard to like me. I'm like I am because I love you, and I love my brothers. This is hard for me as well."

"I get it, Tom. Really, I do. You've got to learn that you're no longer alone. You're the alpha to your brothers, but you're also like my husband, my mate. You've got to learn to share." She touched his cheek before walking out toward Guy.

****

Staring up at the moon, Guy let out a breath. The scent of Kitty invaded his senses, and he turned toward her. She wore a sexy red negligee that highlighted her curves. His brothers were close by but not too close.

The moment she cleared the steps, she ran toward him. Holding his arms out, Guy held her close, and claimed her lips the moment they touched. She sank her fingers into his hair, groaning into his mouth.

"I love you," she said, biting down onto his lip.

Without waiting, Guy took her down to the ground, not given either of them a chance to hold back. He wanted to mate with her, to be inside her. The sooner he did it, the closer they were to being together forever.

"I love you too, baby, so much."

He kissed her long and deep. Stroking his fingers up the inside of her thigh, he teased her slick cunt, thrusting a finger deep inside her. She was already wet, and he wanted to make her dripping before he took her pussy with his dick.

Kissing her neck, he began to tease her clit, stroking over the swollen nub. She opened her thighs wide. The moon was high in the sky, and his wolf was so close to the surface. Guy wanted to mate with Kitty. For the first time since the last moon, he finally knew without a shadow of a doubt that Kitty was his mate. She was the pack mate, destined to love them and to give them children.

"Please, Guy, I need you inside me. Don't make me wait."

He didn't take his time with her orgasm like he had the last couple of weeks. The moment he got her into bed after the end of the claiming he'd have her panting for release for hours until he finally gave her one.

Moving down her body, he sucked her clit into his mouth. Her taste exploded onto his tongue, and he wanted more. No, he needed more. He needed enough to let him survive two more moons before he got a chance to be with her again.

Flicking her clit with his tongue, he fucked his fingers inside her, bringing her closer and closer to orgasm.

She didn't last, and with the sound of her orgasmic cries ringing in his ears, he aligned his cock to her entrance, sliding deep within the walls of her pussy.

"You feel so good," Kitty said, sinking her nails into his arms.

"I don't want this to end." Tears filled his eyes

knowing what came next.

"Oh, Guy." She cupped his cheek. "I love you, and I trust you. I promise, this is the start of something amazing." She lifted up, kissing his lips passionately. "There's nowhere else I'd ever want to be than with you and your brothers. You're my life."

Pulling out of her tight heat, Guy made love to her. He didn't fuck her. With his lips against hers, he took his time, prolonging the mating, and loving the woman in his arms with all of his heart.

Only when he couldn't hold out any longer did he make the sacred mating vows.

"Kitty Evans, you are mine as I am yours. Nothing will tear us apart. I mate with you. Please accept my life and my protection as yours."

His cock swelled inside her, making him groan at the intense pleasure of the moment. They were bound together as mates, husband and wife.

"Yes, I accept your claiming and your love." She lifted up, kissing his lips. "I'm ready." She tilted her head to the side, and he sank his canines into the flesh of her neck, relishing the taste of her blood. The wolf within him howled at finally discovering his mate, the one woman who was supposed to be his for the rest of their lives.

Pulling away, he made a cut against his neck, drawing her close so that she could take his blood, completing the claiming. His brothers came close, each of them licking her blood and forever binding them all together as one united pack. They were all close, feeling the need to mate with her, but they must wait their turn.

All but Stuart moved away, and Guy began to rock inside her. Her slick pussy made it easy for him to glide in and out of her warmth. Kitty held onto him, loving him.

Holding her close, Guy didn't want to let her go.

"I don't want to stop," he said, whispering the words.

"We have to, Guy. Two more moons and we'll all be safe." She looked into his eyes, and he found himself drowning. "You helped me. I love you, and we can do this."

Slamming into her, Guy couldn't hold off his orgasm. He held her tighter than ever before as his cum spilled inside her, filling her up.

"I love you. I will always love you," he said.

His orgasm subsided, and still he held her.

"Guy?" Stuart asked.

Looking into Kitty's tear-filled eyes, Guy shook his head.

"Turn, Guy. Turn and run. I'll be fine."

He eased out of her body. His heart was heavy as he moved away from her. She kept smiling, nodding her head. Before he could stop himself, he turned into a wolf before her eyes, and took off into the woods. When he looked back he saw Stuart sat beside her, stroking her cheek. It wasn't enough as far as Guy was concerned. He'd have wrapped Kitty in the safety of his arms and never let her go, but he wasn't his brother.

"You've got to trust Stuart," Tom said, following him.

Shaking his head in wolf form, Guy took off.

Two more moons to go.

Epilogue

Stuart carried Kitty up to his room. She was passed out from the mating claim. He placed her on his bed, and simply stared at her. Her beauty took his breath away. Touching her hand, he locked his fingers with hers even though there was no grip to her hand.

This was his moon now, and he was scared.

He'd never been good with women. They were good for one thing, fucking, and he'd always been more interested in his books.

With Tom being the alpha, the one in charge of finding their mate, Stuart had lost himself in books to ease the fear.

Now, it was up to him to mate with Kitty.

He didn't see a problem with anything other than his own fears. He was attracted to her, but he'd never been great with women, never needed to be, and books were his escape from the fear of failing.

"You better treat her like a princess, Stuart." He turned toward the door to see Guy standing there, looking pale as fuck.

"I'm going to."

"She deserves your attention. Not your damn books."

"Fuck off, Guy. I'll do my part, and I'll love Kitty with every part of my being."

"You better, otherwise, I'll burn you with your fucking books if I have to. Teach her some of the shit you read about. Be the hero she deserves."

Guy closed the bedroom door, leaving him alone with Kitty.

Staring at the blonde beauty, Stuart knew in his

heart he'd do the best he could.

The End

SAM CRESCENT

STRONGEST PASSIONS

The Pack Claims a Mate, 4

Sam Crescent

Copyright © 2015

Chapter One

Kitty lay on the bed sleeping while Stuart sat in the corner reading a book. Surprisingly it was a romance book, and he was trying to find the right ways to woo this woman, this goddess who smelled of the pack. Licking his dry lips, he kept glancing up at her. The negligee she'd worn was bunched around her waist, and her hair was still dirty from the ground. The last thing he wanted to do was scare her by taking her for a wash.

Tom, Roy, and Guy had come and visited her to see if she was fine. Each of the three men had asked if he was going to wake her up. Stuart didn't want to wake her up in case he startled her.

Someone knocked at his door, and he knew without a shadow of a doubt it would be Mark and Joey.

Placing his book on his chair, he made his way toward the door. They both stood together, both appearing identical, but their scents were slightly different so the pack always told them apart.

"How is she?"

"She's still alive and sleeping."

Opening the door, he allowed the two men inside. They stopped at the edge of the bed, staring at her.

"Did you know we're going to have to share her?" Joey asked.

"I thought sharing was your thing?"

"It is, but this is a mating. We've got to work hard for her to accept the both of us," Mark said.

"Usually we just fuck the woman who falls at our feet, no questions asked." This came from Joey.

"Look, we're all feeling the pressure right now." Stuart rubbed the back of his head wishing with all of his heart that he could say something that made total sense to everyone. He came up blank. This was what he hated, not knowing what to say to make everyone feel better.

With all the books he read, he should be able to make everyone feel better, yet it seemed all he did was make everyone feel worse. No one trusted him, Guy being the main brother who believed he was going to fuck this up.

He didn't realize he was speaking until Mark and Joey each put a hand on his shoulder. "Don't do it, Stuart. We're all in this together, and we have every faith in you."

"Books are so much easier to handle. They don't expect anything from me other than to be read."

"You know a book doesn't have a personality, right?" Joey asked.

"They've helped me get through the darkest times of waiting for Tom to make a choice." He shrugged. "I do what I have to do."

They all turned to look at the blonde haired beauty sleeping in his bed.

"I can't believe she stood up to Tom, demanding she be here," Mark said.

"If anyone is ever going to stand up to him, it'll be our mate." Stuart was proud of her for standing up for what she believed in. He didn't understand why each moon of the claiming she had to be away from the rest of the pack. It made a hell of a lot more sense to him for her to remain with the whole pack, restoring and guaranteeing the bond for life. But what did he know? He was only the fourth brother down the line. He didn't know anything, not really.

"She's so beautiful," Joey said.

"She smells amazing." This was from Mark.

"You better get going before she wakes up and is scared when she sees three wolves staring at her."

"We're in our human form," Mark said.

"It doesn't matter. I don't want her afraid." Stuart ushered them out, closing the door. When he turned back around, he saw her eyes were open, staring back at him. In a horror movie it would be completely eerie. "You're awake."

"They think I'm beautiful."

He moved to sit beside the bed. "You are beautiful, Kitty."

She smiled. The moment her eyes fell away from him, something hard and deep hit him in the chest. He didn't like her looking elsewhere.

"Are you hungry?" he asked.

"A little bit." She looked back up at him, and the beast within him calmed.

"Okay, I will go and forage in the fridge. Erm, the bathroom is through there if you want to wash or something."

"Thank you."

She didn't show any sign of moving.

"I'll go and get us some food." He left his bedroom without a word. Walking toward the kitchen, he saw all of his brothers sitting around, nursing cups of hot chocolate.

"How is she doing?" Guy asked.

"She's hungry, and sad." He walked toward the fridge.

"And you left her? Stuart, I swear if you screw this—"

"I'm not going to screw it up, but yeah, I got the memo. If I do screw it up, you're going to make me wish I was never fucking born. I get it, and you don't need to keep yelling at me. I get it." He yelled the final part so that Guy understood that he comprehended every single word he spoke.

"You've left her alone."

Stuart let out a sigh and stared at each of his brothers. He didn't know how much time had passed as he just stared at them. Guy went to say something else, but Tom stopped him.

"I left Kitty alone so she could get some time to herself," said Stuart. "Having six men around all the time is going to be hard for her. She'll need her own time, and her own space, where she can curse, and argue, and not give a shit that six men are close by. I'm not failing her or the pack, Guy. I'm giving her time." He grabbed several plates of meat, cheese, and bread. Placing them on the counter, he started to assemble two plates of food. "She's just spent the past month with you, and two other brothers. She's hurting, and I get that you're worried. Why don't you trust me to do what is right?"

He glared at Guy, hoping his older brother saw the pain he'd inflicted, even if he hadn't meant to. Stuart stared at the plates wondering what else he'd need for her to eat. Glancing at the clock he'd noticed twenty minutes had already passed with him arguing with his brother, and arranging food on a plate.

"You've got to learn to trust me," he said, fed up with the lack of his brother's trust.

"I'm sorry. I'm worried about it. I shouldn't have threatened you."

"No, you shouldn't have." Stuart finished with the food. "Now, I'm going to take this up to Kitty." He left without saying another word.

****

Padding into the bathroom, Kitty winced at her reflection. She looked a mess. Her hair was all over the place, and her body was covered in earth. There was also dirt under her nails where she'd gripped the ground beneath her.

She'd been awake when Mark and Joey had each tried to console Stuart. Lying on the bed, listening to him talk about his fears, she'd understood it was hard for him, just like it was hard for her.

Climbing into the shower, she washed away the night's claiming even while Guy remained in her heart. She'd seen how hard it was for him to walk away.

Two months to go.

The first month had already started, and she could handle two more months of being with three men. She'd never actually been part of a threesome, but she could do it. For the love of the pack, she'd do it.

Once she finished in the shower, she wrapped a bath towel around her and went back to the bed. It was filthy, and she got to work, stripping the bed, then placing on new sheets, which she'd found in the bathroom on her hunt for a towel. Sitting on the bed, she stared around the space. It was rather plain with six different ceiling to floor bookcases. She walked over to the shelves and started to look through the books. Not every book she stared at was a fiction book. Tilting her head to the side, she read the titles, seeing several cookery books and multiple books on crafts and buildings.

He had a variety of interests.

Grabbing a book on cookies, she moved toward the bed, to open them up. Several pages were dog eared, with a small flap pulled down. She began to open the book to look through the recipes that he'd noted on. Most of them were filled with chocolate and oats.

The door opened, and she glanced up.

"I hope you don't mind." She held the book up for him to see. "I love cookies."

"No, I don't mind. I'm not going to go mental because you've touched a couple of books."

"You're the bookworm."

"We all have hobbies that keep us from going crazy."

"Are these recipes you like?" she asked.

"No, they're recipes I'd love to try. I'm not very good in the kitchen. I burn toast."

"The best cooks burn toast."

"No, I set fire to my toast, and we had to change the stove because the fire got out of control. Believe me it wasn't very good. I am, however, allowed to empty the fridge out of fresh produce." He held a tray that was loaded with two plates.

Her stomach rumbled for a taste of the food. "It looks delicious." Closing the book, she reached out for her plate. Stuart placed the tray on the bed, then grabbed a pillow from the corner, and placed it over her lap.

"The plate is cold."

"How is everyone?" she asked, thinking about all five brothers waiting downstairs.

"They're nervous that I'm going to find some way to fuck this up." He smiled, and she found herself smiling back at him.

"I'm not going to bite."

"You love my other three brothers."

"I've spent time with Tom, Roy, and Guy. Give me time and I'll come to love you."

"Four weeks isn't really a long time."

She saw his doubt. "Do you think it's hard to love you?"

"No, I'm a realist, and real life isn't what it's like in the books. I don't expect you to fall in love with me." He was breaking her heart.

Picking up a slice of cheese, she kept her gaze on him, wondering what she could say to him to make him see reason.

"Do you want to learn how to cook?" she asked. For someone who wasn't allowed to cook, he had a variety of cookbooks on the shelves. Kitty wanted to reach out to him.

"I'm not allowed in the kitchen. My brothers barred me from going in."

"Is that the only thing stopping you?" She took a chunk of chicken and took a bite.

He shrugged.

"Stuart, work with me. I know you want this to work as much as I do. Please," she said, begging him.

"After each claiming you've always been so depressed. I wanted to give you a chance—"

She pressed her fingers against his lips. "I'm going to stop you there. Yes, I'm upset. I didn't understand what was going on, but now I do and I'm not going to let anything ruin our time together. Give me a chance to love you."

His tongue peeked out, and she gasped as he licked her fingers. "You taste like chicken."

Kitty started to laugh seeing a playful side he clearly kept hidden from his family. "Now, do you want to learn how to cook?"

"I do. You're going to need to clear it with Tom and the others."

"Okay, where do you think I can find them?" she asked, climbing off the bed. She wanted to do this with Stuart.

"They're downstairs."

"Is that down to your wolf senses?" she asked.

"A bit. I can sense where they are."

She nodded. "I'll be back, promise." Glancing down at her body, she shook her head. "Well, I can always use my body to get what I want."

Stuart laughed, and she left him while he was still laughing. Kitty loved the sound. Rushing downstairs she found all five brothers in the sitting room watching a horror movie. Rolling her eyes at the big breasted blonde, she cleared her throat. The television was turned off, and they all turned around to look at her.

"Glad I've got your attention. I've been talking with Stuart, and I was wondering if you'd lift the ban on the kitchen so we could make something together. Something sweet?" She gave them all her most dazzling smile.

"Sure," Roy said.

"Absolutely." This from Tom.

"Can't wait." Guy spoke up next.

Mark and Joey spoke at the same time. "Looking forward to it."

Smiling, she rushed into the room, giving them all a hug. There were definitely going to be some perks to having six men who loved her.

Chapter Two

The following day Stuart woke to Kitty in his arms. She was still snoring slightly, and he found the sound utterly adorable. Everything about her was adorable. When she'd walked into the bedroom after getting the agreement from his brothers, she'd been so damned happy. He couldn't bring himself to ever hurt her.

The last three months had been a nightmare for him. His wolf yearned for the woman who was currently lying in his arms. Stuart had never felt like this for any other woman in his life. He'd been happy to fuck willing women and then leave them.

Reaching out, he slowly pushed some of her blonde hair out of the way. She really was a beautiful woman. After she'd eaten most of the food he'd brought up for her, she'd brushed her teeth, then settled into one of his shirts before climbing into bed. She'd tapped the bed like it was the most natural thing in the world.

"Morning," she said, opening her eyes. She quickly placed her hand over her mouth.

"What's the matter?"

"Morning breath. I need to go and brush my teeth."

She was gone before he got a chance to stop her. Laughing, he climbed out of the bed, and followed in behind her. She was flushing the toilet then washing her hands. Leaning against the doorframe, he admired her body, and the little glimpse he got of her curves as she moved just from watching her made his dick ache with the need to be inside her.

He moved in behind her, reaching the top shelf in order to hand her a toothbrush. "There you go."

"Why do you put everything on the top shelf?"

she asked, muttering.

"We get the chance to see your ass." He glided his hands across her cheeks, emphasizing his point. "I'll put everything you need on the top shelf."

She was staring at him in the mirror. Her eyes were wide as she stared at him. The scent of her arousal flooded the bathroom. His wolf perked up taking notice. He released a little growl, and Kitty moaned. Wrapping his hand around her waist, he pulled her against him. The toothbrush was forgotten as he held her close, pressing his dick against her ass.

Placing her hand over his, he was shocked when she started to push his hand down to land between her thighs. She wasn't wearing any panties.

Cupping her pussy, he slid a finger through her wet slit, finding how aroused she actually was.

"Fuck, you're already soaking wet." Stuart couldn't believe she was turned on by him. With her already experiencing three of his brothers, he really didn't think there would ever be one fated female for all of them. Yet Kitty was soaking his fingers.

"Touch me, Stuart."

She reached around, pushing her hands into his pants, and circling his dick. He hissed as she moaned. Slowly, he worked his fingers between the sweet flesh of her cunt, loving the smell of her. He couldn't help it and needed to taste her.

Lifting his fingers to his lips, he sucked his digits into his mouth, moaning at the taste of her. She was musky and sweet.

"So good, it feels so good, Stuart."

Staring in the mirror, he watched her face as he went back to touching her pussy. Slipping two fingers inside her sweet cunt, he pushed his thumb against her clit, watching her eyes close. Not once did she let up on touching him. Her hand moved up and down his shaft, drawing him close to orgasm with her touch alone.

"You feel so good, Kitty. I can't wait to touch you. To get my dick inside yo—" He stopped before he could finish saying exactly what he wanted to say to her.

"What is it?" she asked, slowing down her hand.

"Nothing."

"Don't hide from me, Stuart. Be natural with me. Be yourself." She began to thrust her pussy onto his fingers. "Please, it'll only work if we're natural with each other. Please, I want your touch. I love your fingers inside my pussy."

He took her at her word, working her pussy. "I want to throw you to the bed, pull you up to your knees, and fuck you so hard you can't walk straight."

She moaned, and her cream soaked his fingers.

Kitty liked what he was talking about? It was too good to think about.

"Yes, I want that," she said. "I'm so close."

Stuart was going to blow at any moment. Kitty was driving him crazy. Her fist squeezed him tightly. He imagined this was how tight her pretty pussy was going to be.

"Come for me, baby. Come over my fingers so I can lick them clean."

He pinched her clit, soothing out the slight pain by stroking over her nub.

"Yes, yes, yes," she said, screaming each word out. When she found the peak of her orgasm, he slammed his fingers into her cunt while also teasing her clit.

Kitty didn't stop working his cock. Watching her come apart was all it took for him to find his own release. His cum exploded into the sweatpants he wore.

When it was over, he held her tightly. They were both shaking. Pulling his fingers from her tight pussy he licked her cream off his digits, moaning as he did. Stuart couldn't look away as Kitty removed her hand from his pants, lifting her cum-smeared hand for him to see. With her gaze on him through their reflections in the mirror, she licked the cum off her palm.

"Do you have any idea how damn sexy you look?" he asked.

"I guess I look kind of hot."

"Damn right you do."

He didn't know how he was going to survive a month with this woman being in his bed. What scared Stuart more was being able to do what Tom, Roy, and Guy had been able to do, and that was to give her to his next brother.

Mark and Joey better be ready for her when the time came.

****

Later that day Kitty giggled as Stuart had his cookies stuck to the work surface. He'd been so cocky in rolling out his dough with how perfect and flat it looked. Kitty had taken the time to flour the surface, and to move her cookie dough around. Now it came to cutting out the shapes, and Stuart's were losing all kind of shape, looking a mess.

"Okay, so I guess I should have followed your instructions."

"I thought you knew best," she said, laughing. He looked so cute blushing.

"What's going on in here?" Guy asked, walking into the kitchen.

She kept laughing. "Stuart's got all of his cookie dough stuck to the work surface, and he's going to have to start again." She hummed as she placed all of her cookies onto baking trays. Once she was finished, she gathered up Stuart's dough into a ball, splitting it down.

"Do you want to have a go?" she asked, looking toward Guy.

"If Stuart doesn't mind."

"I don't mind. This is a bloody nightmare. I want to make cookies, not have to get tools from out of the garage to pry it off the work surface." Stuart wiped his brow with the back of his hand. "This is actually a lot harder than it looks."

"It's not. You're making it complicated." She started to instruct him once again, telling him slowly what to do. He rolled out either way, then sprinkled flour over and under, turning it slightly before doing the same motion. When his cookies were at the right thickness, she handed him the cookie cutter, and then another cutter to Guy. While she pulled hers from the tray onto a cooling rack, Guy and Stuart filled the remaining trays. She placed them in the oven. They all worked side by side to wash away the mess they'd created.

Kitty giggled as Stuart poured water down her back.

"Hey, don't. Those cookies need to stay edible," she said, when Guy went to throw some water at her as well.

The scent of the baking had lured in everyone else. Tom, Roy, and the twins sat at the table.

"I'll get the kettle on." She was loving her time with Stuart. It had only been a morning, but she saw something deeper within him. Kitty adored his humor and his hands. He'd touched her body that morning, and she'd come to life. There was so much more to Stuart than the books he read. He was hiding in them, almost afraid to come out and play. She wouldn't let him stay hidden. When she opened up the pot that held the tea bags she saw it was empty. "I'll go and fill this up." She left the room, going into the storage room just off the kitchen. Turning on the light, she looked over the shelves until she found the bag.

"You're good for Stuart," Guy said.

She turned around to smile at him. Moving toward him, she pressed a kiss to his lips. "Thank you for the most amazing claiming last night." From the moment she'd seen him last night he'd looked guilty, and she hated that. This claiming was going to tear them all apart, but she wasn't going to let it happen. Kitty was going to make sure they all stayed together.

"I'm sorr—"

"No. You've got nothing to be sorry about. I love you, and you made me open my eyes and realize it's not just me suffering. All of you are. Stuart, he's scared just like you. This means so much to all of you. I really hope I don't let you down." She pressed another kiss to his lips. "Now, let me make a cup of tea so that I can finish these cookies."

"Thank you," Guy said, his voice filled with emotion. She looked back, smiling.

"Why?"

"You're bringing my family together. The claiming, it has been something we've wanted and yet dreaded at the same time. You're making us all come together. I can't thank you enough."

As she touched his cheek, tears welled in her eyes. "I've got a family again."

Leaving the room, she made her way toward the kitchen. Stuart was waiting, nibbling on a cookie, which he quickly hid behind his back when she came into the room. "The idea is to have some that we can ice so they're awesome." She shook her head, placing the pot on the counter.

"They taste amazing," Stuart said.

"They'll taste even better with icing." She

finished off the tea, then went to the tray of cookies that she'd gotten out of the oven first. Nearly ten of the cookies were gone. The men were covering their mouths, chewing. She wasn't angry. In fact, she couldn't help but laugh.

Grabbing the icing sugar from the baking cupboard she'd spotted a couple of nights ago, she picked up the meringue powder then the sugar.

While the guys were watching her, she made up the icing, filling pastry bags, and handing one to Stuart. For the next hour, she began to decorate the cookies with Stuart close beside her. Each time their arms touched, she found herself getting more and more aroused by his closeness. She had to cross her legs because the arousal was simply getting too much. Out of the corner of her eye, she saw each of his brothers had gotten up to leave.

"I can smell you, Kitty," he said.

She took a deep breath, finishing off her cookie. Standing up, she glanced toward him. "What are you going to do about it?"

Chapter Three

Grabbing Kitty's hand, Stuart pulled her close, banding his arm around her waist. He lifted her up onto the table away from their cookies. Slamming his lips down on hers, he groaned as she opened her lips for him to explore inside her mouth. She tasted like the butter cookie he'd seen her eat. Not that he was complaining. He'd taken plenty of the butter cookies for himself.

He untied the strings behind her neck, tugging the apron from her body. Next came his shirt, which she'd borrowed that morning, then his sweats. In seconds he had her butt ass naked spread open on his table. Running his hand up and down her body, he touched every inch of her.

"You're so beautiful."

"Everyone keeps saying that."

"It's the truth. When it comes to you we all speak the truth. You've got to believe us."

"I do." She gasped, crying out as he leaned down sucking onto her nipple. He didn't take his time. Stuart moved from one nipple to the other, stroking a finger between the lips of her pussy.

Biting down onto her nipples, Stuart couldn't wait to be inside her.

Stepping back, he unbuttoned his jeans, pulling out his thick cock. Stuart grabbed her hips, turning her over so that she had her back to him. He opened her thighs, finding her entrance. Sliding his finger through her pussy, he teased her cunt until she was dripping.

Gripping the base of his cock, he pressed the tip against her pussy and slammed right deep inside her.

"Yes," she said, screaming out. Anyone in that house would know exactly what he was doing. In that moment, Stuart didn't give a fuck what his brothers heard. Her pussy was a fucking dream, tight and hot, and everything he wanted.

Gripping her hips, he slammed within her harder each time. Slipping his fingers to her clit, he began to play with her sweet little nub, feeling her come apart in his arms.

"That's right, baby. Come all over my dick."

"Stuart, something tells me you're rather naughty."

He gripped her hair into his fist, pulling her head back. Stuart didn't answer her with words but actions, pounding into her pussy and playing with her clit at the same time. He didn't stop either. Over and over, he rammed inside her, hitting a spot so deep that it had her gasping, screaming his name.

It was what he wanted to hear, what he needed to hear, his name being screamed from her.

"Do you want to come, baby?" he asked.

"Yes. I want to come. I need to come. Please, Stuart."

He loved hearing her beg, but he wanted her to come over his dick before he found his own release. Each of his brothers had fallen for this woman, and so, too, was he. She was everything they'd always wanted, always dreamed about. When Guy entered the kitchen and asked to join in, there wasn't any hesitation from her. He didn't feel angry or jealous when Guy went into the store cupboard with her.

This was what it really meant to be a pack, bonded together. Before Kitty came along, they'd been six men that were thrown together because they were born to the same man and woman. Kitty gave them a reason to be together.

She united them.

Releasing her hair, he grabbed her face, turning

her so that he could touch her lips. He licked along her bottom lip, then pressing his tongue into her mouth. Stuart slowed his pace down for her to get used to his invasion. Like all of his brothers, Stuart wasn't a small man. He was large, and he wanted Kitty to know he could satisfy all of her needs, even those she didn't know she had.

She came all over his naked cock, her cum washing over his length. He didn't stop stroking her clit or kissing her. Stuart fucked her while prolonging her orgasm. She came a second time before he found his own release.

By the time it was over, they were both panting, and he slowly released her clit. She cried out, shuddering in his arms.

"Wow," she said. "I'm the luckiest girl in the world."

Her cheeks suddenly heated.

"What's the matter?" he asked.

"What if they heard us?" She bit her lip, looking left and right.

"They left the house. Don't worry. After the full claiming they don't give us privacy."

"They won't?"

"No, knowing my brothers they'll join in and have you screaming out." He pressed another kiss to her mouth.

"I think the icing is dry," she said, surprising him.

He burst out laughing, unable to contain himself.

"You're probably right." He didn't want to pull out of her body. With his dick going soft, he acted quickly, turning her around and picking her up. "I'm not done with you yet. I want to fuck you again and again."

He carried her upstairs to his room.

"They always say watch out for the quiet ones.

They weren't lying, were they?"

"We all learned to do different things. I've always loved books," he said.

"Why?" She pressed kisses down his neck toward his rapidly beating pulse.

"Why do I love to read?"

She nodded.

"If we didn't find the right woman we were going to be lost to our wolf. Guy told us that there are no longer any secrets between us. Anyway, I thought I would be forever trapped by my wolf. I never really thought I'd get the chance to read."

"So you read books because you thought you'd stay a wolf forever?"

"Yes. I didn't want to miss the chance to have known another world. In books, any book, you can be anywhere while sitting at home. I wanted to have as many memories as I could make in case the worst happened."

She didn't laugh at him. Instead, she cupped his cheek, staring into his eyes. "I love you, Stuart."

"And I love you."

****

Three weeks passed with so much ease that Kitty couldn't believe it. She was inside the main library, with a hell of a lot more books, staring out of the window. Stuart was a man filled with passion, love, and loyalty. He loved her, and the pack, and he had one insatiable appetite that she loved as well.

Guy had been so worried about him, and yet Stuart had been so wonderful. He rarely picked up a book unless she asked him to read to her. Stuart could go all night long. His passion in the bedroom was insatiable, and he loved to experiment, bending her this way and that. She did remind him one night that she wasn't a wolf but a human.

Pulling her knees up against her chest, she stared at Mark and Joey training with Tom. Every morning without fail all the men did over an hour of training and practicing their fighting moves. At first she'd thought it was hot to watch. Now, she found herself wondering what would happen if they were ever attacked. Stuart had told her they trained in case of an attack. There were more packs out there, and it was something their parents had done before them. It was better to be prepared than to never expect anything to happen, and be taken by surprise.

"What's the matter?" Stuart asked, coming into the library. He closed the door, moving toward her.

"Nothing."

"I can't lie to you, so you can't lie to me. Don't keep me in the dark, baby."

She laughed. "I was worried." Turning back to watch Mark and Joey, she saw Tom take both men easily to the ground.

"What are you worried about?"

"Life. I worry about not being good enough for you all. All of those concerns that mere humans suffer."

He knelt beside her, staring out of the window.

"We all worry just like you," he said.

"I doubt that."

"There's six of us to this pack, Kitty. Some packs have more; some have less. We're worried we're asking too much of you. Not many women would love to be with six men regularly."

"I've fallen in love with all of you. Even Mark and Joey. You're all a family, and I want to be part of that. What happens if I lose one of you? I don't know if I can bear it."

He wrapped his arms around her, pulling her in

close. She loved it when he held her tightly. It was these moments when she felt close to him.

"It's time we got you out of this house. Come on, let's go and watch a movie."

"How's that getting out of the house?"

"We're not watching a movie here. Come on." He took her hand, leading her outside. Kitty waited by the truck while Stuart ran toward Tom. They spoke for a few minutes with Tom looking toward her.

She jumped into the truck only when Stuart started to jog back toward her.

"Is everything okay?" she asked.

"It's fine. I was just clearing everything with Tom that we're good to go." He climbed into the truck, turning over the ignition. She was excited about getting away from the house. It was a beautiful house on a large plot of land, which was all amazing. She needed something different though. Kitty needed to be part of the world, as otherwise she was going to get scared of stuff that was outside. "Sometimes being in the house can make the whole outside world terrifying. I'm taking you out to prove to you that you've got nothing to fear."

They cleared the gates of the house and were on the main road. Stuart tapped his fingers on the steering wheel, humming to himself.

"Thank you," she said.

"For what?"

"For bringing me out."

"You can thank me once we've seen a movie. I can't guarantee that you're going to like what's showing at the movies. Do you want some music on?"

"No."

"Talk to me, Kitty."

"I'm just nervous."

"We're almost at the end of our month together,"

he said.

"Yes. Then Mark and Joey will have their month."

"The twins are anxious to get their hands on you. They want to make you their mate as much as my brothers have. We all want to move on so we can just share you, love you, and be a family together."

She swallowed past the lump in her throat. "That's all I want as well."

He glanced over at her, and she was already smiling back at him. "I hope I haven't bored you too much."

"You don't bore me, Stuart. You're an amazing man. You need to stop hiding behind those books and be part of everything."

"I've not scared you then?" he asked.

"You've not got it in you to scare someone." They parked in the town, and she noticed how busy it was. The house had air-conditioning, but the heat was sweltering outside of his car. Stuart offered her his arm as they started walking down the street. She glanced around seeing the grocery store, a small mall, and a diner. At the end of a long road of shops was the movie complex.

"We're not an overly busy town, but we make do." They crossed the road. Stuart waved to several of the locals on his way toward the complex.

"You know a lot of people."

"Tom likes to keep to himself, but I like to get to know people. During my early years I could always be found in one of the rooms at the library. I've also spent a great deal of time chasing girls. My older brothers don't know about it. Mark and Joey do as we're close in age. I spent a lot of time talking to everyone." They entered the movie complex, and Kitty glanced up at the short list of movies playing. None of them were on her to-watch list, but she wasn't going to demand to go back to the house. This was her first trip out with one of the men since she was first taken. She told him one of the tear-jerking romance movies that she had yet to see.

Stuart didn't laugh. He paid for their admissions, and sat beside her, complete with popcorn and all.

Chapter Four

After the movie, Stuart wiped the tears from under his eyes and made his way outside. It was already getting dark. They had sat through three movies, and he'd turned his cell phone off when Tom had called after the first one finished.

"Oh my God, I didn't expect that ending. It was so amazing, and I did shed a tear, so you can cry." Kitty pushed her hand through his, and they walked toward his truck. "I loved today, Stuart. It has been the best day ever." She stared up at the sky. Her eyes looked animated, and he was simply pleased to be the man who'd put that look into her eyes.

He turned his cell phone on to find multiple missed calls and several texts. Glancing through them, Stuart chuckled as Tom began to call him.

Answering the call, he raised a brow at Kitty before talking.

"Why the fuck haven't you answered any of my calls? Do you know how worried I was?" Tom was yelling, and Stuart had no choice but to hold the receiver away from his ear and the shouting.

Kitty took the cell phone from him. "Hey, Tom, how are you doing?" Before Tom could even start talking, she continued to finish what she was saying. "I loved today. We saw three movies, and even though I really didn't want to watch any of them, I loved them. You should have been here. I told Stuart to turn off his cell phone because it kept ringing. Was it you?" There was silence for a few seconds while Tom talked. "Well, I'm sorry we made you wait. The movie was so good. You should have seen it."

On and on it went.

"We're on our way home now. Have you eaten?

No, okay, we'll sort that out. Bye." She closed his cell phone, handing it over to him once she climbed into the car.

"Is he going to kill me when I get home?"

"I don't think he's going to kill you, but he may be a little pissed off with me." She shrugged. "I loved today, and I don't care how worried he was. They could have all driven to town to find us." She rubbed her hands down her thighs. "Right, we're getting takeout. What do you think, Chinese, Mexican, or fried chicken?"

"Chinese," Stuart said.

He pulled the truck up to the Chinese restaurant. They walked in together and ordered enough to keep them fed for a couple of days. He was starving, and if Tom had been doing his pacing, it could only mean that he'd be starving.

Stuart paid for the food while Kitty carried it back to the car. It wasn't long before they were pulling up outside of the house. Roy was cutting logs. Tom was sitting on the steps, watching them. Mark and Joey were sparring, and from the looks of it, Guy was playing on a video game.

"Do you think he rounded them up to come and upset us?" she asked.

"I don't know. Just be your usual charming self and we'll get out of this scot free." He turned the ignition off and climbed out of the truck. Stuart took the food from her so that she could climb down.

"Hey, guys," she said, smiling at each of them. "We had the most wonderful time."

He followed behind her carrying the box of food while Kitty talked over and over about everything that had happened. He couldn't help but smile when she did her swooning voice of one of the main men.

Tom glared at him while the rest of his brothers

smiled. Kitty had always been happy. Well, for the most part she'd been happy. But she hadn't been like this, talkative, and vibrant with life.

She removed her jacket, grabbing plates. The more she talked, the more the men fell for her. Stuart didn't doubt he was going to get a warning from Tom. He'd gladly take it for her.

They sat down around the large table in the kitchen. Kitty opened up boxes and served them all some dinner while leaving the bites in the boxes for them to take. She sat beside him, eating.

Glancing around the table, he saw how contented everyone was at being near her. This was what she did to them, awakening them all from a sleep none of them knew they were taking.

After they finished eating, Kitty went to take a shower while he stayed down to do the dishes.

"You should have called," Tom said, the moment it was safe for him to argue.

"I didn't have time. Kitty took all of my attention. We watched one movie after the other. We ate popcorn, used the toilet, and sat through more movies."

"I was worried."

"Tom was worried that you wouldn't bring her back," Mark said, taking the plate from Stuart.

"I wouldn't do that. You've got to learn to trust me."

"I didn't think that. Don't start, Mark."

Mark stuck his tongue out. Rolling his eyes, Stuart finished doing the dishes with Tom and Mark, while his other brothers finished putting away the uneaten food.

"You've got one week left until the claiming," Tom said.

Stuart let out a breath. "I haven't forgotten."

"When you've claimed her, Mark and Joey will claim her, and then that will be final. She'll be our claimed mate completely."

"Will you back off and relax when that happens?" Stuart asked.

"I hope you know we were all worried about you sticking to your role within the pack."

"I read, Tom. I'm not stupid. I know I had to mate with Kitty, and I will continue to mate with her. I love her with all my heart. She's part of the pack, and I've already seen what she does for all of us. She unites us, Tom."

His brother and alpha smiled at him. "I'm sorry. I guess it's hard for me to back down at times."

"You've got to learn to. Otherwise it's going to cost you. Kitty won't take any of your shit."

With that, Stuart left the kitchen, making his way up to his room.
****

"Did they hurt you?" Kitty asked.

Stuart laughed, closing his door. She was so turned on, and she had hoped he wouldn't make her wait long for him to arrive. He never did disappoint her. She brushed her hair, trying her hardest to act nonchalant.

"No, he didn't hurt me. I may have snapped at him. Tom may be licking his old wounds."

"At least we know he can heal."

She licked her lips, and gave him her back.

Be casual, Kitty.

Turning back to look at him, he was frowning at her.

Dropping the towel, she stepped toward him. "I need you, Stuart," she said. "I need you now." Running her hands up his chest, she circled her arms around his neck, and pulled him in for a kiss. She moaned, licking his lips before sliding her tongue deep into his mouth.

"Fuck, baby."

"Don't hold back, Stuart. Fuck me hard like you want to."

He shoved her to the bed, and she stared at him as he tore his clothes, making quick work of getting naked. She loved the way he looked without any clothes. He was so damn hot.

When he was naked, he gripped his cock, working his hand up and down the large shaft. The tip glistened with his pre-cum, and she released a moan, wanting to taste him.

"Suck my cock, baby."

Crawling to the edge of the bed, she went to touch him, but he slapped her hand away. "No, I don't want your hands. I want your lips. Suck me into that pretty mouth. Show me that you want me."

Opening her lips, she stared up into his eyes as he slid his cock into her mouth. She moaned, closing her lips around him, and sucking him hard.

Stuart released a hiss, and she loved the sound. He was trying not to lose control, but with her mouth on him, he was losing the battle.

"Do you know what you're doing to me?" he asked.

She hummed "yes" around his shaft.

"Fuck, that feels so good. Your mouth is perfect."

Kitty bobbed her head onto his shaft taking as much of his cock into her mouth as she could.

Suddenly, he pushed her off his cock, pressing her back to the bed. Before she could ask why, he was between her thighs, licking and sucking at her clit.

She cried out, screaming for more as he licked her pussy. The pleasure was out of this world, delightful, scary, and yet one of the best things she'd ever experienced.

"Yes, please, suck my clit." She stared down watching him circle her clit then slide down to fuck into her pussy with his tongue. Over and over he did this heightening her arousal.

She didn't get a chance to come. Stuart pulled away, moving onto the bed. He landed between her thighs, running the tip of his cock through her slit. Biting her lip, she took several deep breaths then screamed as he slammed to the hilt within her. He was so big and long she was shocked that she was able to take him.

"That's it, baby, take my cock, fucking love me taking you."

"Yes, Stuart, I do. I want you to fuck me. To take me."

"The claiming is a week away," he said.

"I know, and once the whole claiming is finished, we'll be together, and we won't be on a deadline." She couldn't wait for everything to be natural with the whole of them. Kitty was growing tired of constantly fighting them and the claiming. When it was over, she was going to take her time with each man without the time limit of the full moon.

"Please, Stuart."

He slammed every inch of his cock inside her, and Kitty screamed out her pleasure, loving the feeling of being full of him.

"Yes, Kitty, such a nice tight pussy." He pulled out of her only to slam back inside. Stuart did this for several thrusts, taking her harder than ever before.

Her orgasm started to build, but Stuart didn't let her reach her peak. He pulled out, flipping her onto her stomach, and tugging her ass up against him. Stuart slid his cock back into her pussy. His fingers delved between her thighs, touching her clit. He got his fingers nice and wet drawing them back.

She tensed up as his fingers started to tease the puckered skin of her ass.

"Sh, relax, baby. I'm not going to fuck you here, but I am going to play."

Kitty took several deep breaths, closing her eyes as he stroked over her ass lighting another fire within her.

"Yeah, baby, fuck back onto my cock."

She began to thrust back against him, taking more of his cock inside her pussy. At the same time, he pushed the tip of one finger into her ass. The pleasure was out of this world, shocking her to the very core of her being.

"Mark and Joey are going to fuck you together, lay their claim."

Kitty couldn't wait. She'd be lying if she said she hadn't thought about it. She thought about everything and the endless possibilities these men inspired within her.

"Your pussy has gotten all nice and wet for me. You want to be fucked in the ass?"

"Yes." She wanted everything that made them happy.

"Good." He began slamming inside her pussy leaving his mark exactly like he promised.

The sound of flesh hitting flesh permeated through the room. She reached between her thighs touching her own clit. Kitty couldn't hold back another moment. She fell into her orgasm as Stuart grunted out his, filling her pussy with his cum.

"I love you, Kitty," he said, kissing her shoulder.

She believed him. She really did.

Her only wish now was for the claiming to be over so she wasn't ordered who to sleep with.

Chapter Five

The night of the claiming was once again here, and Stuart walked out of the house and stared up at the full moon. He didn't want this night to start or to end. Shock filled him as he glanced down to find Kitty already sitting on the ground staring up at the sky. All five of his brothers were gathered around, watching her. Concern shone on all of their faces. They were not used to her being ready before any of them.

He wondered how long she'd been sitting there while he'd been taking the time to get ready.

Stepping toward her, he knelt down on the ground. Her knees were up against her chest, and her gaze never once wavered from the sky above them.

"Baby? Are you okay?"

"I'm fine, Stuart."

"You're here early."

"I didn't want to wait around. I was shocked when I was the only one, but then slowly, you all appeared. You're the last one." Finally she turned her head to look toward him. "Do you want to mate with me?"

The tension in the pack mounted at her question.

"Of course I want to mate with you. I love you."

She smiled up at him. "I love you, too."

"What's going on, Kitty?"

"I don't want this month to end. I've not wanted any month to end, and I'm scared that once it's all over everything is going to change."

"The only thing that's going to change is we're all going to love you at the same time. You're not going to know a moment's peace because of us. There's six of us, and we're all desperate to make this work with you. We all want to make you happy, adorn you with gifts and love. Maybe one day, have children of our own?"

"I'd like that. It's what I want for us. For all of us."

He stroked her cheek, pressing his lips against hers. "Never doubt my love. You've given me a chance to shine, and for that, nothing is going to take away what we have with each other." He kissed her lips once again, then again, sliding his tongue inside her mouth as she opened up to him.

She wrapped her arms around his neck, pulling him down to the earth.

Stuart chuckled, cupping her large breasts in his palm and running his thumbs across each of her distended nipples.

"I love your hands on me, Stuart. I love everything you do to me, but today, I've got to be the one in charge."

"Then ride me, baby. Take what you want."

Kitty lifted her silk negligee over her head, exposing the beauty of her tits and naked pussy. She worked the sweatpants he'd worn down his body until he lay naked for her to enjoy.

"This is how I want you," she said, grabbing his cock. She licked along the side of his dick before pulling him into her mouth.

He groaned, lying back on the grass and staring up at the sky. The full moon was high in the sky, and he stared at it while Kitty loved his cock. He loved the way she sucked on his dick, taking him to the back of her throat. Sinking his fingers into her hair, he changed from looking at the sky to where Kitty sucked on his cock.

When he couldn't stand anymore he tapped on her head, telling her to slow down or to ease up.

"You've got to stop or I'm going to come and spoil the claiming."

She crawled up his body, gripping his cock in her fist. "It's okay, Stuart. I'm more than ready for the claiming." She sank down onto his cock, groaning out.

He gripped her hips, thrusting up at the same time, and loving the feel of his pussy clenching him.

Together they found a slow pace that had him hitting to the hilt within her.

"Yes, Stuart, fuck me, make love to me. I want this. I want the claiming, and when this is all over, we'll spend more time."

No, he wasn't going to let her think about the next month. He was going to take her and have her begging.

Quickly changing their positions, he pulled out of her pussy, pushing her to her knees, and sliding back inside her. He wrapped his fist around her hair, tugging her back. The heat of the pack and the height of the moon were helping the beast within him to take over.

Slamming into her pussy over and over, he licked over her pulse.

The balance of power had changed, and he was the one in charge. "That's right, baby. I'm the one in charge. The moment I get you alone, I'm going to fuck your body raw."

She panted and gasped, her pussy clenching around his cock as he fucked her harder than ever before.

"Touch your pussy. I want you to explode over my dick. Let me hear you, Kitty."

Her fingers began playing with her clit, and Stuart groaned as the walls of her pussy seemed to tighten around his cock.

"That's it, baby. Give me your cum. I want it over my dick before I blow inside you." He nibbled on her neck, biting down hard on her ear.

She gasped, crying out, and her hand worked her

pussy a lot harder.

"I'm coming, Stuart."

Pounding into her pussy, Stuart felt his own release mounting. "Kitty Evans, you are mine as I am yours. Nothing will tear us apart. I mate with you. Please accept my life and my protection as yours."

He bit down onto her neck right over her pulse and kept slamming inside her.

"Yes, I accept your claiming and your love." She panted out the words. They were only loud enough for him to hear. He pulled away, pressing his wrist that he'd just cut, to her lips. She swallowed him down, and he came within the tightness of her pussy.

His brothers came closer, taking her blood and cementing the bond. With each moon, the connection to Kitty strengthened. He felt her release, her need, her fear, and her love for all of them. This moon had given them all an insight into her feelings.

It was over too soon. Tom's voice invaded his mind, and Stuart held onto Kitty not wanting to let her go.

"Go, Stuart, you've got to go."

He held her a little tighter, and glanced up as Mark and Joey stepped forward. "Take care of her. Love her."

"We will." Both brothers spoke in unison.

Nodding his head, Stuart pulled away from her, walking into the forest before changing into his wolf. He left her behind, hating the fact he had to wait another moon before he could truly call her his.

****

Kitty finished brushing her hair on the bed. She'd not wanted to pick either Mark or Joey's bed after they'd carried her inside. This room was her own, and her own clothes were inside the walk-in wardrobe.

Someone knocked on the door, and she called for them to come in. She was surprised to see Tom enter her room.

"Do you mind if I come in?"

"I said you could. This is your house, remember. This is all yours."

She put the brush down. The last few months she'd been wearing negligees or one of the men's shirts. Today she'd settled on a plain pair of pajamas. She felt cold, sad, and lonely.

"This is your house as well."

"I know, but forget it." She tried her hardest to smile yet struggled. "What can I help you with?"

"We're all worried about you," he said, moving closer to her. He took a seat, and all it would have taken was to reach out and touch him.

"Why?"

"We can sense your pain, Kitty. None of us want you to be in pain."

"I can't even have any privacy with my pain?" She climbed off the bed, moving toward the window. Staring out at the full moon, she was starting to hate the large ball in the sky.

"We love and care about you."

"It's hard, Tom. It's hard moving from one brother to another, and feeling that loss as acutely as the last. It brings it all back. I know you're all suffering because of this, and I'm not trying to be a bitch. I just need one night, okay. One night where I'm by myself."

"The claiming is never easy on anyone."

"Why does anyone do it? So far I can't see a reason why people would want to." She folded her arms across her chest, glaring at him.

"It's for the moments afterward. We're all hurt and hurting. This isn't easy for any of us, I promise you.

We're all waiting for the moment when the claiming is over, and we can love without fear."

Tears filled her eyes. Tom moved from the bed, going toward her. He leaned down, kissing her lips while wrapping his arms around her.

"I love you," she said. "Every time we go through the claiming, I'm reminded of when you walked away."

"I'm not a monster, Kitty. It tore me up doing what I did. I hate what I've put you and my brothers through. If it makes you feel any better I'm going to make sure you never know a moment's pain again."

Resting her head on his chest, she nodded.

"I know this is against your rules, but will you have all of your brothers come here? I want to sleep with you all in the same bed."

"That bed isn't big enough," said Tom. Before she could protest, he took her hand, and led her out of her room. "This was something we thought about and so," he stopped talking to open another door, "we got this room set up. The rules are there to guarantee that you bond with all of us. It's what my father told me, and what I've tried to follow, but there's nothing that says you won't bond with all of us, if you share the bed with us."

Roy, Guy, Stuart, Mark, and Joey were sitting on a large be. It was so huge that they had to have made it themselves.

"We can break the rules for this one night. Mark and Joey will share you in your room tomorrow. Tonight, we all just want to hold you." He took her hand leading her into the large bedroom.

She wrapped her arms around his neck, pressing a kiss to his lips. "Thank you."

Rushing to Roy, she kissed him, then Guy. She lingered a little more with Stuart. The guilt in his eyes hurt her deeply.

Next she kissed Mark and Joey, smiling at them. "Thank you both for being so understanding."

"You mean everything to us, Kitty. We can wait one night." This came from Mark.

Joey reached out, linking their hands together.

They all touched and helped her onto the bed. Settling down, she watched Tom turn off the light then make his way toward the bed.

"Do any of you snore?" she asked.

"I do," Mark said.

She chuckled.

"Be careful, Tom breaks wind," Guy said. "He bloody stinks."

Bursting out laughing, Kitty slowly found herself relaxing in the large bed. One month to go and everything would be over. They'd all be mated, and she wouldn't have to fear being left behind by either of the men.

Every now and then someone reached out to touch her. She loved the way their fingers seemed to linger on her skin. Closing her eyes, she inhaled all of their masculine scents. All of men, the whole of the pack were close by.

She was safe in the comfort of their home.

"Love you, Kitty," Roy said. Opening her eyes she saw he was the one lying in front of her.

"I love you."

One by one all six brothers voiced their love for her. She spoke the same words. Reaching out, she cupped Roy's cheek. "It's almost over. We're almost there, and I won't let you down."

All she needed to do was accept two men at the same time. That was what terrified her the most. Could she really do it?

Only the next moon would tell the true tale.

The End

DOUBLE TROUBLE

The Pack Claims a Mate, 5

Sam Crescent

Copyright © 2015

Chapter One

Mark and Joey stood in the front yard glancing up at the house.

"Do you really think this is going to work?" Mark asked.

Joey snorted at his brother. This was a plan for pussies, and at the moment they both wanted to get into Kitty's pussy. When they'd woken up that morning surrounded by their brothers, Joey had felt the challenge of competing against each of them. Tom was the alpha, and he was able to make any woman melt just by listening to his voice. Roy was the quiet and caring one, and no one questioned him. Guy was all action without using many words. From the way Stuart was last night, he was all about the sex and passion. While he and Mark had each other, and there wasn't a lot they did without each other. Their parents had often called them "double trouble".

They could both have Kitty screaming with pleasure between them. Joey didn't want to get straight down to sex. Yes, he wanted to be inside Kitty more than anything, and to leave his mark on her body, but he also wanted to get inside her heart, and he knew deep down that Mark felt the same way. The main part of the Claiming was not only for each brother to fall in love with their mate, but for their mate to fall in love with them. If a pack only had two or three men, that was fine. The biggest problems happened when it was five or more men. Kitty didn't have it easy. Falling in love was almost impossible at the best of times, but they knew they loved Kitty. They were wolves, and their feelings were heightened in ways that Kitty wouldn't understand. Each of them wanted to own a small piece of her heart. Reaching out, Joey stroked behind the little golden retriever's ears. The puppy was so cute and adorable. She'd had her first lot of injections and would be going back to the vet in a couple of weeks for her second lot, so she'd be fine.

"This is a dumbass thing," Mark said.

"It's a cute thing."

Standing outside their home, Joey yelled for Kitty to come to them.

"It's dumb."

"It's cute."

Over and over they argued until Guy was the first one to appear. When their brother spotted the little puppy resting in Mark's arms, he burst out laughing, then stopped, glaring at each of them. "You little shits."

Kitty came out of the house, followed by the rest of their brothers. Roy, Tom, and Stuart glared at them, but Kitty's eyes grew all teary and excited.

"Oh my God, is she for me?" she asked, rushing down the steps. She didn't snatch the dog from Mark's arms. Joey smiled as she reached out to pet the little pup. Like Joey had predicted, the little pup wanted Kitty.

They'd taken one of her shirts to see which pup responded best to Kitty's scent. The one pup that came over, and pretty much went to sleep in her shirt, they'd taken, after purchasing of course.

"She is for you."

"I can't believe you got me a puppy."

Mark eased the little dog into her arms, and Kitty pressed her face against the little pup.

"We thought it would help with the loneliness," Mark said.

"She's beautiful. I can't thank you enough. Really." Kitty stroked over the little pup, who had settled easily into her arms.

Joey was pleased with his idea of getting her a pet. Both of them refused to get a kitten, but a dog, they could all handle around the house. From the glares of their brothers, he knew they'd done the right thing.

"You've got to name her."

"I will. Wow, I can't believe this." She reached out, wrapping her arms first around Mark, then around Joey. "Thank you both so much for this."

Next came the kiss, which Joey was happy with, and so was Mark from the look on his face.

"We've got the car loaded with everything she's going to need. We'll bring it in," Mark said.

"Okay. I've got breakfast in the kitchen for the pair of you." She gave them each another large smile before rushing into the house. Their other four brothers didn't even get a look in.

Joey laughed at the jealousy on their faces.

"I can't believe you went and bought her a pup," Roy said.

"Hey, we've got to get inside her heart somehow. Each of you brought a little something extra to the mix. Mark and I, we had to use something else."

Tom frowned. "You don't need to buy her love with gifts."

"Look, this wasn't about getting Kitty to love us with a gift. She's going to get lonely out here at times. With a dog or two, it might help," Mark said. "We were thinking of her."

"I think it's great," Stuart said. "Did you see the smile on her face? She looked so damned happy." Their bookworm of a brother moved toward the car and picked out several large bags of puppy food.

They all began to bring in the pup's stuff listening as Kitty talked to her. Joey couldn't help but smile at the love already blooming in her eyes from having the pup.

"Have you decided what to call her yet?" Joey asked.

"Yes, she's going to be called Angel. Her coat is so pale, and the way she just sits and takes it all in, she's an Angel."

"Angel it is."

Sitting at the table, Joey waited while Kitty grabbed out his breakfast. He was starting to eat as Mark entered. Kitty did the same, grabbing him some food. Angel started to fall asleep, and Kitty began arranging her bedding, putting the pup down to sleep.

His brothers had disappeared. This was still their mating month, so Mark and Joey needed to be close to her.

"I missed you both this morning."

"Sorry about that. We wanted to do something special for you," Mark said.

Joey shot his twin a smile. They'd woken up wanting to do a hell of a lot of things to Kitty. Instead, they'd decided on the pup.

"She's called her Angel."

"Great."

"Thank you so much." Kitty moved around the kitchen kissing first Mark's cheek, then his. "I really don't know how to thank you enough."

"Keep kissing us like that and we'll call it even," Joey said.

Kitty took a seat between them. Her gaze flitted over each of them then back at her cup. She looked nervous, and it didn't sit well with Joey for her to be nervous.

"What's the matter?" he asked.

****

After the sweet gesture the twins had shown her today, Kitty didn't want to say anything to dampen the mood. When she'd woken up that morning to find them gone, she'd felt alone. Now, seeing as they were getting a gift for her, she felt bad.

"It's nothing. I was just wondering how this is going to work?"

"How what is going to work?" Mark asked.

"This between us. I've, erm, never been in a threesome let alone—God, this is embarrassing. I mean, I'm sleeping with six brothers. It seems so damn surreal to be even saying I've never been part of—oh just stop me from talking."

Both men were laughing at her.

"We're going to take this slow or as slow as the mating month will allow."

She felt like a dork. The last four months she'd been with four different men, yet she was nervous about the twins.

"We know it's hard for you," Joey said.

"It's okay." She glanced toward Angel, charmed that they'd bought her a dog. "Thank you so much for buying me a puppy. I've never had a pet of my own."

Damn, Kitty. They've probably been with more

experienced women than you.

Angel popped her little head up, yawning and rolling over. Kitty giggled, getting down on the floor to play with her. Mark and Joey didn't disappear like she expected. They joined her while she was playing. They were passing a small ball between them. Angel was rushing around going onto their legs.

Kitty loved it, and when Angel needed to go outside, she moved toward the door.

"The owner did say they were trained," Mark said.

All three left the house, following after Angel. The small pup didn't rush to the forest. She took her time exploring the gardens close to her. Kitty kept her gaze on Angel but leaned back. Mark wrapped his arm around her shoulders while Joey linked their hands together. This was right to Kitty. Their warmth washed over her, surrounded her, and made her feel safe. It was one of the things all the brothers had in common. They all left her feeling safe. Both of these men were going to have to share her, and it was the thought of what was happening *during* the sharing that made her nervous. She'd never had anal sex, and she didn't want to have it anytime soon. But the last thing she wanted to do was to fail her mates. She loved all of them.

The day wore on, and she loved every second of it. At nine o'clock that night, Kitty excused herself and made her way up to her room. This was going to be where Joey and Mark came to her. She was nervous with both men. They were used to sharing their women while she wasn't used to sharing anything.

After taking a long leisurely bath, she climbed out, and made her way into the bedroom in time to find Mark already half naked. His hair was damp from having a shower.

"Where's Joey?"

"He'll be here soon. You don't need to worry."

She held the bathrobe tight around her. Modesty was a waste of time. They had all seen her naked in the past few months. Last night they'd seen her submit to Stuart's brand of passion.

"I'm not worried." She pushed all of her personal doubts aside. Mark and Joey were no different from their brothers. They were the same. Both men looked almost identical, but Kitty could tell them apart. Mark had slightly darker hair than Joey, and Joey was mostly the quiet one. He was reaching out to her, and she appreciated it.

Stepping toward him, she dropped her towel, and saw the hungry look that passed across his face. "I think it's time we stopped being nervous around each other," she said.

"Two men is a lot to take," he said.

"I know, but I'm going to have six men, Mark. I'm not going to lie to you. I'm worried about taking you both. I shouldn't be worried, I know, but I am." She ran her hands up his naked chest, relishing each smooth contour of muscle. He really was a sculpture of male perfection.

"We're going to make it good for you, Kitty. I promise." Mark gave her a reassuring smile, and she couldn't help but respond to him.

"There's no rule book to say I can't learn how you liked to be touched or kissed while we wait for Joey."

"We don't have to share you until the night of the full moon, Kitty."

"Then why are we afraid to explore each other?" She ran her fingers across his breast, moving down to tease the opening of his jeans. Glancing up at him, she bit her lip, trying her hardest to tempt him. "Do you want me, Mark?"

"Yes. More than you could know."

Kitty took hold of his hand and placed it over her breast. "Then touch me, baby. Touch me and show me what you want."

He took over cupping her breast. His other hand grabbed her ass pulling her closer to him. The hard ridge of his cock pushed against her stomach. She arched up, wrapping her hands around his neck.

Arousal spilled from the lips of her pussy, and she heard him take a deep inhale.

"Fuck, you smell so damn good."

"It's all for you, Mark."

"Now that is fucking hot," Joey said, entering the room.

Both of them turned toward the new arrival.

"Don't mind me. I'm going to take a seat and enjoy the show."

Kitty smiled as she watched him lower into the chair in the corner. Joey was also dressed in a pair of jeans and nothing else. Both men weren't wearing any shoes either.

Turning her attention back to Mark, she glided her hand down the front of his body, pushing her hand into his pants to feel the soft skin of hard cock.

He was big. She couldn't wait to see him completely naked.

"Her ass is so fucking big and ripe," Joey said. "Show it to me."

"She's nervous," Mark said.

"She's got nothing to be nervous about. When we take her together, she'll be more than prepared. We're not going to hurt you."

Mark turned her, running his hand all over the

THE PACK CLAIMS A MATE

cheeks of her ass. Their arousal was only deepening hers, making it hard for her to focus on anything else.

"I can smell how damn hot she is. She loves your touch," Joey said.

"And she loves you watching, don't you, Kitty?" Mark asked.

"Yes to everything. I love your touch, and I love him watching." Kitty didn't know how she was going to survive the month. Both men already had her soaking wet from the talking between them. She couldn't wait for them both to be naked and ravishing her.

The claiming moon couldn't come soon enough to her.

Chapter Two

Mark groaned as she leaned down and sucked on one of his nipples. He sank his fingers into her hair, watching her. Out of the corner of his eye he saw Joey pushing his jeans down to expose his cock.

Her fingers wrapped around Mark's cock and started pumping his length. Taking hold of her hand, he gently shoved her away.

"There's only one way this is going to go, Kitty, and that's with me in charge." He tugged open his jeans, letting them drop to the floor in a heap. "Sit on the bed."

She slowly eased down on the bed. Her eyes kept darting from his cock to his face.

"With the way she keeps licking her lips I think she wants a taste of you, Mark," Joey said.

"Do you want to suck my cock?" he asked, wrapping his fingers around his exposed length.

"Yes, I want your cock."

"Then open those sweet lips and show me how much you want it."

Kitty opened her mouth, and he stepped closer, presenting her with his long shaft. She was so beautiful he couldn't believe that he and his brothers had gotten so lucky. Pressing the tip of his cock into her mouth, he groaned as the wet heat swallowed him down.

Gliding his fingers through her hair, he watched his cock disappear within the recess of her mouth then reappear. His dick was coated with her saliva, and he couldn't recall ever seeing a more welcoming sight.

She moaned around his length, and the vibration only increased his arousal. He was so near to orgasm that he withdrew from her mouth. Without saying a word he pushed her to the bed and dove between her thighs. He sucked her clit into his mouth, moaning as the taste of her cum exploded on his tongue.

He lapped her up, plunging his tongue into her tight pussy. Moving up, he circled her clit, tapping the swollen nub over and over again. The bed dipped, and out of the corner of his eye he saw Joey join them. With his tongue still on her cunt, he watched Kitty reach out, touching his twin. They were joined as one on the bed.

"Such a pretty mouth," Joey said, sliding his dick inside her.

Fucking his fingers inside her, Mark tongued her clit repeatedly. Within seconds she came on his fingers, and he licked up her cum, loving the taste of her.

Joey groaned in the background, pumping his dick into her mouth. Mark climbed up her body, aligned the tip of his cock to her entrance and slammed inside. She released Joey to scream and beg.

"That feels so damn good," she said, thrusting up to meet him.

He gripped her hips, watching her, unable to look away from the beauty that she was displaying.

Pulling out of her warm heat, he stared down at where they were joined. His cock was slick with her cream, and he wanted to fuck her harder. Joey looked like he was at the brink of his control.

Reaching down, Mark fingered her clit, bringing her to a second orgasm as he found his first, filling her sweet pussy. Joey found his own release in her mouth, and afterward they were left wrapped around each other and panting on the bed.

"That was mind-blowing and amazing," Kitty said.

Climbing onto the bed, Mark wrapped his arm around her waist as Joey held onto her hip.

"Kitty, I know my brothers have already told you this, but I do love you," Joey said.

"I love you, too."

Kissing her neck, Mark told her the same. He did love her. The whole pack was in love with her. During the last mating it had opened the connection so they were able to sense her feelings. He didn't like her hurting and would do everything in his power to make her happy. She was the only woman he'd ever cared about.

"Do you two share women often?" Kitty asked.

"No, not as often as you're probably thinking," Mark said. "We've shared women, and you'll be the last one we share. I don't want another woman."

"Me neither," Joey said. "You're in here, baby." He placed her hand over his heart.

Mark continued to kiss her neck, and she shuddered in his arms.

"So, do either of you have any hobbies?" Kitty asked.

"I don't read like Stuart," Joey said.

"I'm not asking about Stuart." She snuggled between them. "I'm asking about you."

Mark chuckled. "I like watching movies."

"And I like working out." Joey flexed one of his muscles.

"While we're out here we have to make our own entertainment. It's not always easy. There's the vegetable patch, and there's the general work on the house." Mark and Joey had always done things together. They loved watching movies, and working out. They also were the ones responsible for the furniture that had been made within the home. Mark loved working with wood and creating some fine works of art, even if they were used within the home.

No one complained or got a splinter.

Joey said as much while Mark simply thought about it.

"So, what are you going to do with me for the next month?" she asked.

Tightening his hold around her waist, Mark smiled while looking at Joey. "I think we can come up with something."

****

Joey stepped out of the way as Kitty fell to the floor from a high kick that had her collapsing onto her butt. She was dressed in workout clothing, and he and Mark were taking turns training her. Kitty had asked for them to share their loves and their passions with her. Working out, sparring was part of who they are.

They were teaching her ways to defend herself while also making it as fun as it could be. Tom, Roy, and Guy were watching. Joey had noticed that Stuart kept looking up from the book he was reading. All of them were loving Kitty's smile, her energy.

It was the last moon, and then they'd all be together. He couldn't wait for the stress to be over.

"This isn't fair," she said. "You're all ganging up on me."

Each of them laughed at the pout on her lips. Mark moved to help her up, locking their fingers together and pulling her up. The moment their bodies touched Joey's cock thickened. Kitty pressed herself against him, running her hand up and down his chest.

Mark growled, and Joey moved in behind her. Her hair was bound up, and he pressed his lips to her neck. While he kissed her neck, Mark claimed her mouth. One of her hands wrapped around Mark's neck and her other gripped his hip, tugging him close. He wanted to throw her to the ground and fuck her so damn hard. Instead, he bit her neck playfully. Now was not the time to spill blood.

"Nice try," he said, whispering the words against

her skin.

Stepping back at the same time as Mark, he laughed at her little growl. It was the most adorable sound he'd ever heard. Angel popped her head up from where she was lying, letting out a little bark as well.

Glancing around at his brothers he saw each of them were struggling with their arousal and had made an excuse to leave. Tom stayed the longest. The yearning in his gaze was easy for anyone to see. He wanted to be with Kitty again.

They all did. Leaving her alone to mate with them was making it hard on all of them.

"He's struggling, isn't he?" Kitty asked when Tom finally disappeared in the home.

"Yes, it's hard for all of them."

"I hope I'm enough to satisfy you." She tucked some hair behind her ear, showing them both how nervous she, in fact, was.

"You've got nothing to worry about," Mark said. "Now, raise those fists and show me what you've got."

She giggled, and any doubt that could have been there disappeared.

Joey left Mark and Kitty to spar and made his way back into the house. He wasn't shocked to see his four brothers at the window watching.

"Her ass is perfect," Stuart said.

"She's perfect." This from Tom.

"We've got a couple of weeks to go and she'll be ours, Tom," Roy said.

"I don't know how much longer I can stand to hold back. You're a better man than I'll ever be," Guy said.

"Traditions and rules are made to be followed. I'm pleased she put her foot down and put me in my place. Having her here during the claiming makes it easier," Tom said.

"Were you ever tempted?" Joey asked, making them all look back at him.

"Was I ever tempted to what?" Tom folded his arms over his chest.

"Not let tradition rule us. Were you ever tempted to join in? To be part of it?"

"Always. I love her, Joey. The only reason I've held back is because I don't want to risk ruining our one chance of happiness. It's hard, but I've got a couple of weeks to go."

Joey was ashamed of touching her outside in front of his brothers. Tom had waited the longest out of them all. Joey wouldn't know what it was like to finally claim her and then leave her for another brother to take his place.

"I'm sorry."

"For what?"

"For touching her. For loving her," Joey said.

Tom moved toward him, placing a hand on his shoulder. "Never apologize for loving her. Kitty isn't mine. She doesn't belong to me. She belongs to each of us to love. I've got no problem with you touching and mating her. She's a beautiful woman, and all women need to have a man who dotes on them. For Kitty, she's got six men. Never be sorry for loving our woman."

Nodding, he moved toward the fridge in the kitchen. He grabbed out three sodas before making his way outside. Mark was having his palms hit by the wild woman. His brother wasn't in any kind of pain, but Joey scented Kitty's exhaustion. She was starting to get tired from the self-defense classes. They trained every single day, and it wasn't a problem for them to spend hours upon hours at a time sparring. Kitty was still only human.

"Break time," he said, lifting the bottles up.

Kitty kissed his lips, taking a bottle, and flopping down onto the ground. Angel came rushing toward her, settling against her mistress's side.

"I'm so tired," Kitty said, wiping at her brow. "How can you do that all day?"

"We're big and strong warriors," Mark said, hitting his chest.

She giggled, sighing after taking a long drink of her soda. "This place is so beautiful. I love it here."

"We love you being here," Joey said, taking a seat on the floor.

"Is everything okay?" Mark asked, nodding his head toward the house.

"Fine. Everything is fine."

They both knew how hard this was for their brothers. One moon to go and they were all anxious to have the mating completed. Tom's wolf had been growing more dominant each day, yet when Kitty arrived and the claiming started, Tom seemed more himself. There were not many growls, or curses, or even changing into a wolf. Joey had noticed that Tom had changed regularly into a wolf over the past year. He'd not warned his brothers for fear of what it would mean.

Since the claiming, Tom had turned only once. It had to be a good sign that the claiming was working. He'd heard of packs failing to find a mate and being forced to split their skin to the wolf within them. The last thing Joey wanted for the pack was for all six of them to be victim to the beast that ran within their veins.

Chapter Three

Kitty lay on the ground in the forest staring up at the sky. Mark was on one side, and Joey was on the other. "It's so beautiful out here." A week had gone by, and she'd come to find the attention from the two brothers to be the most amazing moon claiming she'd ever spent. She loved each of the brothers equally, but it hadn't been like this. Mark and Joey stopped her from thinking about everything she'd gone through. They helped her forget about the past and the pain she'd experienced.

The claiming had been hard on her, yet it had brought them all closer together.

"It is."

"Do you want to have children?" Kitty asked, talking to both of them.

"Yes." They both answered in unison, and she giggled looking left then right.

"How many kids do you want?"

"Twenty."

Again, they both answered at the same time.

"Twenty?"

"We've always wanted a big family. I know our brothers want a big family as well," Mark said.

"Wow, twenty children. Are you sure?"

"Yes, there are six of us. I think we could handle twenty kids."

"What about me?" she asked. "How can I handle twenty kids? I'm only human."

Joey and Mark each took their hand. They were lying on a blanket with an empty picnic basket at the bottom of their feet. Angel was sleeping on Kitty's stomach. They'd taken her to the vet to have her last injection, and Kitty couldn't bring herself to leave her.

The small pup weighed a little bit, but it was nothing that Kitty couldn't handle.

"During the final mating you're going to change a little bit. Mating to six men allows their mate to do what nature intended," Joey said.

"How will I change?"

"You'll be stronger. Nature allows our woman to adapt to having us. You'll be stronger, and be able to nurse twenty children if you wish."

"I hope I make a great mother."

"You will. You've got an instinct for caring about someone," Mark said. "You're going to make an amazing mother, and all of our kids are going to love you."

She believed him.

"Besides, you can always threaten them with those cookies of yours," Joey said. "They're so damn tasty. You could threaten them and tell them if they don't do as they're told, no cookies."

"You're a bad man, Joey. Anyone ever tell you that?" she asked.

"Hey, it would work for me." He squeezed her hand a little tighter. She squeezed him back, leaning her head on Mark's shoulder.

"We're going to have to go inside soon. There's a storm coming, and Tom's going to go out of his mind with worry," Mark said.

"Can we stay a little longer?" she asked.

"Just a few more minutes. Tom will have a search party out for us."

"A search party? He'll round up your brothers," she said, giggling. She imagined Stuart coming out of his book to hunt for her. He'd probably spank her for being a bad influence.

"Whatever thought you're having, I like it," Joey

said.

"I was thinking about Stuart spanking me." She turned to look at Joey, laughing when he made a disgusted face.

"Ew, I'm not liking that."

"No, I was thinking about how he'd want to punish me for drawing him out of his book."

"Well, let me change my first comment. Whatever you're thinking about, I like the way it's turning you on. You smell so fucking amazing." He leaned in close inhaling her neck. "Fuck, Kitty. I'm so damn hot for you right now."

And just like that, she was getting hot for him.

Angel shuffled on her stomach, drawing her out of her arousal. Before they could do anything about their arousal, she had to first get back home.

"Come on, we'd better get back home. I don't want to listen to Tom go off on one of his long speeches about how we should all know better." Picking Angel up in her arms, Kitty waited for the men to finish packing up their picnic. She kissed Angel's head. Her pup settled back into her arms, clearly tired.

They made their way back to the house, and on their way back, the rain started to fall. She removed her light jacket and placed it over Angel but didn't lose pace with Mark and Joey. The moment they left the clearing she saw Tom, Roy, Guy, and Stuart heading toward them.

"You know to come home when there's a storm. A lightning storm is headed our way, and you know how dangerous they can be," Tom said.

"They're dangerous for everyone," Kitty said.

"More so in the forest, Kitty. In the forest people end up dead. Lightning striking one of the trees, explosions, you name it, you could have been killed. It's why our house is far away from the forest." Tom reached out taking her arm.

The anger was emanating from him. Kitty didn't try to fight him. She was trying to fight the shock his touch had created. His fingers had grazed the skin of her arm, and she bit her lip to try to stop a moan.

Once they were inside the house, Tom pressed her against the wall. "I love my brothers, Kitty, and I love you."

Before she could stop him, his lips were on hers, ravishing her. Angel was between them, and she couldn't reach out to touch him. Mark and Joey stayed behind Tom, neither fighting nor protesting. Her body heated at Tom touching her again.

Finally.

They were so close, and it wouldn't be long until they completed the claiming. She'd have Tom in her bed once again.

"Fuck, baby, don't ever make me panic like that again."

"You kissed me," she said, trying to make sense of it.

"Yes. Baby, the last couple of months have been so damn hard, but make no mistake, I won't be waiting for much longer. You'll be our woman to love, to fuck, to share, and to spend the rest of our lives making it up to you."

He kissed her once again, then left her staring after him.
****

Mark sat in the kitchen with Joey waiting for Kitty to come down for breakfast. Ever since Tom had kissed her, they could tell Kitty had been on a high. Glancing over at the calendar, Mark saw they had over a week to go until the claiming.

"I've never been this close to a woman before," Joey said.

"I know."

"We can't fuck this up."

The house was empty apart from him, Joey, and Kitty. Angel was sleeping in her basket. He'd never known a more well behaved pup. She really had enhanced their life. Mark adored her, and he'd seen all of his brothers taking the time to pet her, even Stuart, who would have her on his lap while he read to her.

"We're not going to fuck this up. We know what's needed of us, and we've been working on it," he said.

They had been getting her used to having them both in her bed at the same time. She loved it when one of them was in her mouth and the other in her pussy. Neither of them had touched her ass, and they had to prepare her to take them.

"I bought the anal kit," Joey said.

"Wow, this is a weird subject to bring up for breakfast," Kitty said, entering the kitchen. She wore a pair of boxer shorts along with a vest shirt. Her blonde hair was around her head, and she looked exhausted. "Anal kits." She moved toward the coffee machine and poured herself a cup. "Where is everyone?"

"They went out grocery shopping," Joey said.

"So what is it about these anal kits?" she asked, leaning against the counter. She was nervous, even though she was trying not to be.

Mark couldn't keep his gaze away from her body. The boxers hung off her hips, but the vest shirt she wore showed off the heaviness of her breasts, her waist, and full hips. He reached down to move his cock to a more comfortable position.

"I've bought one for you," Joey said.

"An anal kit?"

"Yes."

"Well, I doubt every girl can say she was given an anal kit as a gift. Why do I have the honor?"

"For the, erm, for the claiming," Mark said.

"Stuart warned me about anal sex." She stopped talking to take a long sip of her drink.

"The anal kit is to help to prepare you for one of—"

"I know what it's used for." She gave them both a small smile. "I guess there's no time like the present." Kitty looked toward the calendar. "There's only a little over a week. We should probably prepare for it."

Guy had marked the claiming by drawing three stick figures in a sex pose.

"We don't have to do it if you don't want to," Joey said.

"I want this claiming to work, so we've got to do it." She pointed at the calendar. "When we have kids, he's not going to be doing that," Kitty said.

"Who do you think it is?" Mark asked.

"My guess is Guy. He's the only one who'd do something like that. I was also here when he drew it. He wanted to cheer me up." Kitty smiled and turned toward them. "So, I've got to take an anal plug?"

"You don't have to be nervous about this," Joey said.

"I am, but I want to be with you guys. We'll give it a try in a moment if you'd like."

Before Mark got a chance to say anything, the door opened, and the sound of all of their four brothers came through.

"We're here with the food," Guy said, shouting out.

Stuart rounded the corner first carrying two bags.

For the next hour Kitty put away the groceries while the men brought them in from the truck. By the time they finished clearing up, and all the groceries had been put away, Kitty had disappeared. Mark and Joey went in search of Kitty to find her in her room. She was naked and lying across her bed. There was a smile on her face, and she rubbed the bed in front of her. "I've been waiting for you both to get up here." She patted the bed. "Do you want to come and join me?"

Mark couldn't look away from the view of her tits. She looked so fucking sexy, and his dick was rock hard. He wanted inside her already.

Closing the door, Joey moved toward the wardrobe.

"Where's he going?" Kitty asked.

Tugging his shirt over his head, Mark smiled. "He'll tell you when he turns up."

Climbing onto the bed, he slammed his lips down on hers, needing her kiss as much as he needed his next breath. He was so turned on, and all the talk of anal kits wasn't helping. Mark loved Kitty's ass. In fact, he loved everything about her.

"Wow," she said when he broke the kiss.

"I love you, Kitty Evans."

"I love you, too." She touched his cheek.

"This is what I was getting," Joey said, lifting up a package.

Mark glanced behind him in time to see the anal test kit along with an extra tube of lube.

"Are you ready for this, baby?" Mark asked, turning back to look at Kitty.

Clear lust shone in her eyes. She obviously wanted the kit, and she wanted each of them. He also saw her nerves over the anal kit.

"I'm ready. I'm more than ready." Kitty sat up,

and Mark helped her move toward the end of the bed.

Joey kissed her lips, and Mark ran his hands down her ass, squeezing her plump flesh.

"Bend over, baby."

Kitty turned her back toward them and bent over the bed. Her nerves were easily scented on the air. While Joey started to unwrap the anal plug, Mark touched her slick pussy.

She moaned, and he easily slid a finger into her pussy. Pumping in and out of her tight cunt, he pinched her clit with his other hand.

"That's so good," Kitty said.

Mark didn't move his hand as Joey moved closer with the lubrication in his hands. "Fuck, baby, I'll take this slow, but I'm not going to lie, you look so damn beautiful."

The claiming was getting closer. Mark felt the need to claim growing higher inside him.

Chapter Four

Kitty moaned as she moved. Joey and Mark had each spent the past week fucking her while also preparing her ass. The first night they'd tried to use the anal kit, but they had failed. It had hurt too much for her, and it had only made her upset. Over the next couple of days, she'd been able to take the kit, and to prepare herself for what was about to happen. The final claiming was happening within days, and she didn't know how long she was going to be able to handle having more than an anal plug in her ass.

Tom was sat in the kitchen watching and chuckling at her.

"Will you stop it?" she asked, growling at him.

"What?"

"Laughing at me."

"I'm not laughing at you."

"Then what exactly are you doing?"

"I'm trying to distract myself so I won't come over there, bend you over the table and fuck you hard."

She paused, turning to look at him. Tom, Roy, Guy, and Stuart were no longer holding back in letting her know exactly how they wanted her. Yesterday she'd been sitting in living room, and while watching a movie, Guy had taken out his cock and started masturbating.

This month was Mark and Joey's, so no one else was touching her, not really. Their presence was only heightening her arousal.

Biting her lip, she moved toward him until she was invading his space.

"We've got days to wait, and then you don't have to hold back." She grabbed his hand and placed it over her breast. Reaching down she rubbed his cock, feeling him swell beneath her hand.

"Fuck, baby." She started to work him up, touching him and wishing Mark and Joey were there to ease her need. "It's a shame I can't do anything about that," she said, moving away.

Kitty didn't stay to see the fallout. She made her way upstairs toward her bedroom. The moment she closed the doors, she climbed on the bed, needing the fabric to be off her body. The anal plug was driving her crazy.

When she was naked, she climbed onto the bed and started to touch herself, cupping her tits before sliding down to finger her pussy.

Some time passed, and her door opened to show Mark and Joey entering.

"Fuck, baby, that is a beautiful sight." Mark spoke first, removing his clothes. It didn't take long for Joey to join in.

Kitty didn't stop touching herself, fingering her pussy while her men undressed. They were so handsome, and it only helped to make her wet.

Mark shoved her hand away, replacing her fingers with his tongue. She arched up into his touch, moaning, whimpering as he sucked on her clit.

"She tastes so damn good," Mark said.

He moved out of the way to allow Joey to have a taste of her pussy. She gripped his cock, fucking the length with her fingers. Kitty watched as he clenched his teeth, clearly struggling with his touch.

"Fuck, baby, you're the best I've ever had."

Her touch was broken by Joey flipping her to her knees. She released a little cry at her world being thrown off balance.

"So fucking sexy."

Hands touched her body, and the arousal and need intensified with his touch.

"Now, this is beautiful."

Fingers skimmed over the anal plug in her ass, and she moaned. The small touch pressed the anal plug a little deeper within her ass.

In the next instance, Joey pressed the tip of his cock inside her, sliding in deep. She groaned. With the plug in her ass, her pussy was tighter, and he felt bigger rubbing against the walls of her pussy. Slowly, her fears about having a cock in her ass were starting to disappear.

The mating couldn't come soon enough. She needed the mating to be over.

"You left Tom in a right state," Mark said, lifting her body up.

His cock was leaking pre-cum, and she licked her lips, needing him within her mouth. She took his cock, bringing him close.

"He wants the claiming to be over, and he wants you, Kitty. We all want you." She loved it when Mark talked. He made everything clear to her, and put everything in focus. "We all love you. You don't have a clue how much you mean to us, but in a few days you're going to know. The connection is going to finally open up, and you're going to know exactly what we want from you, and what we feel."

She couldn't wait.

Kitty believed their words, but at times she couldn't help but doubt just a little.

Joey slammed within her, and she sucked Mark down. She wanted to drive them crazy with need, and to have them at the brink of arousal, which was how they left her.

"Fucking tight, fucking perfect, fucking beautiful. Our woman, our mate, and I love you," Joey said.

"I love you, too, baby. I love you so much."

She moaned.

Mark touched her clit, and it didn't take her long to find release. Her own release sparked her men's release. She swallowed down Mark's while Joey pumped his seed inside her.

Afterward, she collapsed to the bed.

Mark and Joey wrapped their arms around her. This was what she loved more than anything. The moment they found their release they didn't run from her. They each held her tightly against them, holding her close.

"What are you think?" Joey asked.

"I never want this to end."

"What?" Mark asked.

"The love, the touching, the need. I don't want it to end. I hope in fifty years we're still holding each other, loving and never wanting to let go."

"Fifty years is never going to be enough for what we're going to want." Mark tilted her head back and kissed her lips. "You're going to be the most loved woman in the whole world."

She smiled. "I'm going to hold you to that. I'm going to hold each of you to that."

Kitty ran her fingers down Mark's chest before turning to face Joey giving him the same kind of affection.

The moon was near, and Kitty couldn't wait for it to be over.

****

"This is it," Tom said, rubbing his hands together. The full moon was hours away from going high in the sky. Kitty was preparing herself in her room. Joey looked across the sitting room toward his brother. They were both in robes while they waited for the moon to rise.

Kitty was more than prepared for them. The past month had come and gone so fast.

THE PACK CLAIMS A MATE

"We had it easy," Joey said, looking at Mark. "We don't have to walk away and leave her."

"I know. She's going to be our woman," Mark said.

Tom, Roy, Guy, and Stuart sat in the room with them. The anticipation was killing all of them. He didn't know how long he was going to last. Kitty was going to be between them all, shared, and loved.

"Do you have it?" Joey asked, looking at Tom.

His oldest brother pulled out the small velvet box. From the first moon they had all given their opinions on the kind of ring they wanted for her to have. They'd settled on a diamond ring with the words "Snows' Mate" inscribed in the gold.

"I've got it. I'm not going to give up a chance to make this final mating perfect. I want her to feel as special as she's meant to be. Do you think it's, erm, do you think it's going to be okay?" Tom asked.

For the first time in his life, Joey heard the nerves in his brother's voice.

"She'll love it, and we can make it amazing," Joey said.

"We're going to do this," Guy said. "We're finally going to be mated after all this time."

"It's surreal," Stuart said. "She's going to be all ours."

"How did we get so fucking lucky?" Roy asked.

"You waited for the right woman," Kitty said, drawing their attention away from the room and toward where she stood in the doorway. "The moon is high, and none of you were outside." She locked her fingers together. "You've not, erm, I didn't mishear anything, did I? You all still wish to remain mated to me?"

"Yes." All six brothers spoke at the same time.

Joey's heart pounded. She wore a simple, pastel

blue negligee, and her hair was bound on top of her head, cascading around her in curls.

Mark moved toward her first, catching her hand. "Are you ready?"

"Yes, are you?"

"I am."

She turned toward Joey. "Are you ready?"

"You don't know how ready I've been for this moment."

Joey couldn't wait to finally make her their woman, their mated female.

Kitty reached out for his hand. "There's no point in waiting," she said.

Taking hold of her hand, he, Mark, and Kitty made their way outside where the moon was high in the sky.

They were bound together, holding each other's hands. Joey had never been so nervous and joyous at the same time.

All three of them stared up at the sky while their brothers gathered around, creating a circle. This was the final moment that would bind them all together for life.

Squeezing her hand, Joey turned to the beautiful woman who would be his mate and bear children for him and the pack.

"No backing out?" he asked.

"No. I'm not going anywhere." Tears filled her eyes, but they were not the kind of sad tears he was expecting. They were happy tears.

Mark stepped in behind her, kissing her neck. "I love you."

"I love you, Mark and Joey."

"And I love you." Joey cupped her face, pressing his lips to hers. The mating had begun with the moon high in the sky.

Mark cupped her shoulders and brought the thin slender straps of her negligee down her arms. She dropped her arms from where she cupped Joey's face so that Mark could remove her negligee. After it cleared her tits, it fell around her waist.

With his brother's gaze on him, Joey tuned them all out and focused on Kitty. He couldn't think with their excitement about the change about to happen in their lives.

Removing his robe, he watched Kitty's body appear. Cupping her tits, he sucked on her nipples, watching her eyes close as Mark dove his hand between her thighs, teasing her clit.

"You're so wet," Mark said, sucking on the flesh of her neck.

"I want this. I want you both, and it has been driving me crazy needing you both." She gripped Joey's cock, rubbing her thumb over the tip of his cock.

Mark handed him the tube of lubricant that had been stored in the robe. Releasing her long enough to apply a generous amount of lube, he stared into Kitty's eyes.

"I can't wait to be inside you, Kitty. You're like a drug, addictive."

She was turned around before she could say anything.

"We're going to mate you, seal our bond first."

"Okay."

Mark went down to the ground, drawing her down to straddle his cock.

Joey watched as his brother teased her entrance, getting his cock nice and slick with her cream, stroking over her clit at the same time.

Her moans were loud and carried along with the slight breeze in the air. Fall and winter were gaining on them, but by the time they hit, they'd be cemented in their mating.

"Mark, I can't take much more," she said.

Joey watched Mark press the tip of his cock to her entrance, and slowly ease her down on his length. He couldn't recall seeing a more mesmerizing sight. She cried out, gripping Mark's shoulders as she took him to the hilt.

Squeezing more lubricant onto his fingers, Joey settled behind her, slicking up her ass so that she could take him.

The mating call was getting harder to deny. He needed to be inside her, fucking her harder than ever before.

Mark stroked over her clit, keeping his cock still within her.

Only when there was enough lube covering her anus and his cock, Joey started to feed his cock into her hungry ass.

Chapter Five

Kitty cried out as Joey slowly eased his cock within her ass. He stretched and filled her to the point of pain, yet it wasn't painful. She asked for him to stop when the pain seemed to be too much, taking time to get used to the width of him. After a few seconds, she got him to continue. She loved all of the brothers, and didn't want to ruin the mating. Joey stretched her, and it was a combination of pleasure and pain, driving her arousal high, spiking her need for them to just take her.

"So tight, so fucking tight," Joey said.

Mark groaned, rubbing at her clit. They were both joined to her, and it was unlike anything she ever felt. Their touch ignited a flame that only the two men could put out.

She took a deep breath exactly how her men had shown her while taking the anal plug. Pushing out, she felt Joey slide in deep within her ass.

They all cried out, and she could only imagine that the pressure became too much for Mark. His cock seemed to get incredibly hard within her. The pressure built up once again. Joey paused inside her, letting her get accustomed to the length of him inside her.

"Fuck, I can't hold back," he said.

"Then don't. Don't hold back, and fuck me," Kitty said, sinking her nails into Mark's skin.

It took them several minutes, but they soon found a pace that had all three of them drawing closer to orgasm. The brothers moved in closer, and Kitty realized they were seconds away from the claiming. Joey wrapped his fingers in her hair, moving it off her neck.

"Kitty Evans, you are mine as I am yours. Nothing will tear us apart. I mate with you. Please accept my life and my protection as yours." Mark and Joey spoke the words together.

Their teeth sank into either side of her neck, marking her with both of their passion. Their cocks swelled inside her as they took her blood.

Remembering the words she needed to say, she spoke them aloud, clear and precisely. "Yes, I accept your claiming and your love." She sank her nails into Mark's shoulders. They pulled away and pressed their joined palms to her lips. She licked the blood, and an explosion of emotion swamped her. Any barrier she had crumbled down as the mating from the twins sealed the bond among them.

Opening her eyes, she saw Tom, Roy, Guy, Stuart, Mark, and Joey, her pack, her alphas, her lovers. They were all close, licking the blood from her neck. With each brother who tasted her, the bond cemented until Stuart took the last blood.

The love she felt from the connection that had been opened surprised her. They had awakened the bond, their mating.

Mark and Joey grunted as they filled her with their cum.

Kitty couldn't believe what she was feeling. They all loved her, and it was being channeled through the bond, the connection that had surprised her more than anything. She splintered apart with all of her men wrapped around her.

She expected them to pull away from her, so she was shocked when they all gathered her up in their arms, each of them loving and touching her. The connection opened them up together, showing how much love could be shared among people.

Tom held her tightly. Roy kissed her cheek, her arm, wherever he could get his lips. Guy held onto her hand, kissing her knuckles. Stuart stroked her back. Mark pressed against her back along with Joey. Their presence and love made up for the last few months of pain.

"I can feel you, all of you," she said.

"We love you, Kitty," Tom said.

"It has killed all of us to leave you alone."

"None of us ever wanted to leave you alone."

Together they wrapped their arms around her, holding her close.

Later that night when they were all in the mating room, Tom got down on one knee and proposed marriage.

"Marriage? I thought we *were* married?"

"No, this will make us married in the eyes of the law. You'll have everything and be taken care of as my wife. To the pack, you'll belong to all of us."

She took the ring, sliding it on her finger. Her heart melted at the men in her life and in her bed. She'd never been so happy before in her life. "Yes, I'll marry you."

Her men pulled her back onto the bed, showing her exactly how much they loved her.

Epilogue

Twenty-five years later

Kitty looked out of the window to see her eldest son talking to the girl who delivered their paper every morning. She was a good girl, a local girl and only sixteen while her son, Tom Junior, was eighteen.

"Do you think she's their mate?" Kitty asked.

"I don't know." Tom came to stand behind her. It didn't take long for the rest of her mates to join them. Tom, Roy, Guy, Stuart, Mark, and Joey were her mates, the love of her lives, and the reason she'd been the happiest woman in the world.

The last twenty-five years had been amazing. She couldn't find a single complaint with the way she'd been loved by the pack. They had ten children, five boys and five girls, all of them a pack, but her girls would leave and find their own mates in time whereas the boys, they'd find a mate to share together.

"I heard TJ talking," Mark said, which was his special nickname for Tom Junior. "He really believes she is. He can't stop thinking about her. The scent of the girl, everything, it drives him crazy."

"He's flunking math so he can be tutored by her."

"Well, I hope he's found their mate. I wouldn't dream of our boys suffering like you suffered." Over the years she'd learned the truth of what would happen if she'd not mated with her men. They would have been bound to their wolves, never breaking free. The thought of never being around any of her men filled her with so much distress. She hated thinking about it.

Turning around, she smiled at each of them. They all aged slowly, and even she did. She'd borne ten children and yet didn't look a day over thirty. The mating had changed her, adapting her to be with her mates for as long as possible.

"I love you all."

One by one, they kissed and held her tightly, whispering words of love that were so sweet, they had tears filling her eyes. They'd been together twenty-five years, and she couldn't wait for the next twenty-five years to come.

The End

www.samcrescent.com